The First
PERSON

The First
PERSON

PIERRE TURGEON

The First Person was originally published in French as *La première personne* by Les Quinze. It won the Governor General's Award for fiction in 1981.

ISBN: 978-1-926745-41-1

The translator wishes to thank the Canada Council for its assistance.

Cover photo: DreamPictures
Author photo: Léandre Turgeon

Text design and composition: Nassim Bahloul

Book design by Francois Turgeon

Transit Publishing Inc.
279 Sherbrooke West
Montreal, QC
Canada
H2X 1Y2

Tel: 514-273-0123
www.transitpublishing.com

Printed in Italy

Life is a trip in a car—Jim Morrison

For my son, François

DESERTION

Tomorrow, I leave this place forever. All I'll take with me are several changes of clothing, my savings and the picture I took an hour ago of my wife and children. All three of them are waving, as if at the moment I pressed the button they guessed that I was planning to walk out on them.

In the picture, the elder child is eating a Popsicle, his eyes hidden behind his disheveled hair, while the younger one is aiming at me with a plastic Winchester. She must have killed me a thousand times in her imagination. Joelle has her glasses up on her forehead and is smiling bravely, a sort of desperate sweetness in her gaze. They've gone to spend three days with Joelle's parents in Quebec City.

Finding it hard to remain alone here in the deserted living room, I decide to take a walk. The street is lined with bungalows, all more or less identical to my own, skirting the Sainte-Geneviève right down to the River des Prairies. Once again, I am outward bound. It will be a long while before I stop, despite the fatigue that tells me to forget the whole business, to return to the house and stretch out before the dusty screen of the high definition TV. But the street draws me on, with its empty trash cans lying where the garbage collectors tossed them, its clusters of children shouting behind their Plexiglas hockey masks, its cars bleached white by the salt spread on the streets by the roads department. I follow the CN railway line that stretches toward the horizon, passing between high-rise apartment buildings and factories.

I'm not sure where I'm going.

I walk without stopping, effacing forever all that my eyes record, driven by an insatiable need for movement, immersed in my own emptiness, happy not to think, to dominate with my nerve-ends all the past torments of my life. At one point, skirting a skating rink, I slip on the ice and nearly fall, which causes me to break into a nervous laughter. I stop to catch my breath, then remove my gloves and piss in the snow, writing my name in big yellow letters that are almost instantly congealed by the cold.

Up to my waist in snow, I flounder on, my stomach taut with fear, my eyes fixed on the glittering crust from which there emerge a number of strange, interlocking forms: dead branches fallen from the trees last autumn. This silence is alive, speaking to me loudly and clearly.

Gasping for breath, I bend over and rest my weight on my thighs. But in this petrified forest, I am granted no rest. In the heart of so much whiteness, ready at any moment to climb straight to my heart, I exist only through my movements.

***

Back home, I pour myself a cup of coffee and drink it standing in the kitchen, my right hand beneath my belt, pressed flat against my belly, the sleeves of my pullover knotted about my neck. Then, eyes half closed, gaze lowered, I devour a piece of chocolate cake. On the table sit a jug of milk, two empty Coke bottles, and a salt shaker lying on its side. I read the words printed on a cereal box. My fork clutched tightly in my fist, as if about to strike some invisible assailant, I wipe the sweat from my brow.

Lying beneath the blankets, I look through a catalog of merchandise necessary for survival in the far north: rifles, mittens, snowshoes....The telephone rings. It's my father. I make an effort to listen to him without passing judgment, as if I feared he could read my thoughts.

***

I hope soon to reach the fog-bound harbor, where the lapping of waves against the pilings and the wailing sirens of oil tankers will make my flesh crawl. A phantom vessel, I listen to the humming of the refrigerator, my nose buried in the crook of my elbow, my tongue exploring the skin of my forearm, while the emptiness stretches all about me. Will I be able to survive in this extremely rarefied air? Perhaps I was only the echo of all those who hovered about me?

The Tarot cards, spread out on a small table, bear witness to Joelle's patient attempts to predict the future. I bask in the arrival of the night, the two-dimensional pageant of that hour when the sun slowly sinks between a grounded airplane and the control tower of the airport.

***

Forced entry into the small, electronic world of the TV set, the hard sleet of life striking the streaky glass. I click the remote several times: a tour of the world in as many channels. But I can no more reach into that box than I can into my own head. Nothing there to touch, or eat, or love. And yet I've been living in there since I was a child. I recall the snow that fell endlessly on the images of the screen. It was because they had come such a long way, my parents explained; with time, the engineers would correct the problem. And so they did. I dreamed of a color-television future, admiring the sets in store windows, imagining them hanging one day in the sky in place of the sun, their lovely rainbows of colors glowing with an incomparable intensity and purity.

The supreme wisdom is to see the world as an advertisement.

***

I prepare myself a dry martini with several olives. I was incapable of loving my children, just as my parents were incapable of loving theirs. A sad state of affairs that has existed for centuries now. But today we have aspirin. How exasperating: there's only one beer left and Joelle didn't properly recap it, it's gone flat. The last laugh! Holding my thumb over the mouth of the bottle, I shake it to produce a pale semblance of foam. Yesterday, I emptied my bank account. I have scarcely enough money to keep me alive for two weeks. And then? What the hell, I'll hold up a bank! I've already gone into a grocery store with a revolver under my sweater, only to turn and beat a hasty retreat. Bringing that weapon out into the open would have been like undressing in public. Timidity kept me honest. But Joelle's Tarot cards predicted that I would one day find myself confined. In a prison cell?

The firecracker is about to explode. Tricks and Jokes. I never laughed so hard as on that evening I nearly went through the window trying to hit a Ping-Pong ball. "Did you see that?" I asked Joelle. "I was ready to kill myself just to return your service!" I see myself as that cartoon character, that coyote, the instant before he drops into the void. And when Joelle asked me to try to express my feelings without moving a single muscle of my face, I broke up. As I do on all solemn occasions: marriages, burials, official ceremonies—biting my lip till it bleeds.

Whenever I'm asked, "How is your wife?" I reply, "She's all right." I am incapable any longer of distinguishing among the people I meet, they have become all the same to me: a single, neutral, colorless mass, a zero, a nonentity, which somehow goes on functioning. The people I meet are all the same person. The TV informs me that it is 10.40 PM and that the temperature has dropped to -40C.

Searching for my Valium in the medicine cabinet,

I observe multitudes of tiny threads and dust particles floating in the air, capable of causing irritation to my eye if they should slip behind one of my contact lenses at the moment of insertion. This microscopic matter infiltrates even the most hygienic places, originating from the very cloths we use for cleaning. Nothing is truly clean, there are only varying degrees of dirtiness. I like the graceful, unpredictable movements of these minute particles, they remind me of the multitude of whirling atoms and thoughts that must once have come together to form the universe.

***

I bound Joelle's hands and feet. I forced her to kneel. I forbade her to raise her eyes in my direction. I deprived her momentarily of sight, mobility, speech. I loved her. She was so beautiful, she took my breath away.

Instead of fleeing these memories, I must try to find my pleasure, my fulfillment, in them. How difficult it is to give imperceptible things the time they need to reveal themselves! Must think, the tongue pressed tightly to the palate, must produce a truly feminine language, must model, mould. Must become sufficiently detached from myself to allow the possibility of new discoveries. Gradually increasing the speed of the knife about her nude, prostrate body, I drew Joelle to a moment of pure, intense reflection.

***

While eating breakfast, I gaze at the face of a criminal on the front page of the newspaper: hands cuffed behind his back, face raised to the sky, eyes closed, he walks toward a waiting police car. The article speaks of an audacious robbery, the taking of hostages. The suspect was carrying a Colt .45, a perfect imitation of the original, but with a plugged barrel.

In the subway station, I watch the passengers as they flow onto the platform. Our trajectories are as faithful a reflection of ourselves as our mirror images. In each city there are an infinite number of possible circuits, and therefore of lives. Alter your normal morning route, give yourself up momentarily to chance, and you will be instantaneously transformed by your newly defined space. But most people function like robots, and in the great urban motel all the rooms are the same. At the next station, I move toward the exit, clutching an overnight bag that contains my passport, my meager savings and a change of clothes. I stop at a newsstand to buy a pack of cigarettes. Back in the open air, I pull on my coat to protect myself from the melting snow, which gushes in little rivers down the gutters, carrying dead leaves and discarded transfers toward the sewer gratings.

I take the elevator and descend beneath the earth: a series of armored doors, uniformed guards who ask to see my ID. I am back at work, where I operate a computer that receives and codes information from police files all over the continent, its memory coupled with those of other data processing centers in Washington, New York, Ottawa....

The Centre is located at 1568 rue Parthenais, in a bunker 100 meters below street level, beneath the glass and steel tower of the *Quartier Générale de la Sûreté*. It is built to withstand the direct impact of an atom bomb. And it can operate independently of external sources of energy, producing its own electrical power in an emergency by means of a generator. Because it is also equipped with a chemical catalyzer to produce oxygen, it can remain cut off from the terrestrial atmosphere for an indefinite period of time. The cybernetic circuits of my mainframe computer function at a level close to absolute zero, the point at which the total immobility of matter occurs. In the final moment before extinction, they execute operations at a mind-boggling speed, fractionalizing time to its penultimate components. The thought that measures the nanoseconds existed several eternities before it was translated into human words.

Seated before the screen, I strive to become one with the mechanical thought that flies toward the heart of the world. Soon, the aluminum point will slice through the quivering myocardium.

Endeavoring to eliminate the interference resulting from the superimposed codes, I momentarily enjoy an intelligence of a superhuman order. Coupled by fulguration to the entire semantic field of my mainframe, I sense at the back of my brain the inexhaustible torrent of the non-thought of the transistors. I dream of narrative circuits capable of inventing stories, all stories, and printing them with a laser beam at the rate of 100,000 words a second. When I return to myself, it is to find myself in a vastly inferior dimension. Only a few bouts to go before my departure for LA, and that data-processing convention that I shall not attend but which will make it possible for me to fly to the other side of the continent at government expense.

All fluorescent traces vanish from the dusty screen.

A drop of mascara slides beneath the secretary's eyelid. My supervisor gazes angrily at me: he resents the fact that I'm going to California. Soon, he will vanish forever from my life. I've seen too much of his ugly mug, barking orders recorded in the bottom of his plastic larynx. I'm going to abandon him here in his miniature labyrinth. Death might as well come for him right now: the best surprise for him is a non-surprise. I'll be finished forever with this electronic cave and its masses of infractions transcribed from multiple listening tables. The law dealing with family deserters will not result in the mutilation of the exponential aspect of my presence here on this earth. I must be strong! The moral imperative I set myself is never again to acknowledge anything that does not have its origins in uncertainty. This message will self-destruct in exactly 30 seconds.

***

In the cafeteria, they serve me meatballs that I know I won't be able to digest. But the nearest restaurant is a ten-minute walk from here. A lieutenant with a mustache takes the seat next to mine and dips a cracker in his soup. I tell him about a film I saw in which a truth serum was used on a suspect. Does such a drug exist? Indeed, it does. It can even result in the confession of acts that do not exist. Under its influence, a person is no longer able to distinguish between fact and fancy. For example: a man wishes his wife dead, and she is accidentally killed. The man believes himself responsible. The circumstances surrounding the imaginary murder are then suggested to him, and he automatically repeats them in his confession. In fact, concludes the lieutenant, rising from the table, what we have is not a truth serum but a falsehood serum. The truth is not chemical.

***

I return to my board. I have two hours to alter the code of the mainframe. If I succeed, I shall be able to make contact with its memory without anyone knowing, since the program sources and results that the specialists in the Centre work with will remain unchanged. If I fail, I shall never be able to delve into the billions of bytes in the machine again, for the password is changed every day and is not given to absent employees.

My plan, you see, is to become an electronic detective

in LA, using a laptop to make contact with the Centre and obtain information for which my clients will pay dearly. But in order to do this, I must not only short-circuit the password procedure but also erase all my illicit interventions in the daily recording of long-distance data acquisitions. The only solution, as I see it, is to modify the computer's code, built into the machine at the time of its manufacture. I have the clear advantage of having worked for two years as a programmer at the New York headquarters of the company that manufactured the mainframe, a sojourn in the USA to which I owe my children's fluent command of English and my wife's profound hatred of Americans, as well as my own ability to turn to personal, monetary ends a multitude of algorithms theoretically designed to aid in the enforcement of law and order. Too bad I don't work for a bank: I could use my knowledge to increase my personal assets by several million dollars. But I have access to valuable police files containing information that would allow me to blackmail certain political figures and other high-ranking individuals. Alas, I have neither the incentive nor the courage to write threatening letters. Besides, I would then live in constant fear for my life. Of course, by selling information without indicating how it came into my possession I would be well recompensed for the risk.

***

I'm discoursing now in a language that only the microcircuits and I understand, one which precludes all ambiguity and obliges me to think like a machine. I have little time to reflect. If in 30 seconds I do not issue new directions, the mainframe will erase the procedures leading to the central programming core. It's like writing a book that vanishes into thin air the moment you set down the pen. Discovering algorithms that necessitate the use of access codes, I synchronize these with the letters of my name, a procedure that I hope will allow me in the future not only to dispense with the use of a password, but also to erase all traces of my intervention. As usual, the screen indicates the length of time for which my terminal has been functioning.

My throat is dry and my palms are moist. But none of the eight specialists who respond to the police reports received each day are paying any attention to me, and my supervisor has not yet returned from his weekly conference with the police staff. I stare at the ringing of the telephone. I recognize the piping voice of my son:

"I miss you, papa."

Joelle must have dialed the number for him.

"I miss you, too. How's your grandmother?"

"Will you buy me a Popsicle, papa?"

Yes, of course, I reply. And then he launches into a long, complicated account about wolves and guns.

"You're not going to kill me, I hope?"

"No, papa," he replies. "Tomorrow..."

Joelle interrupts to wish me bon voyage.

I'll leave her no note of farewell, for my departure has been motivated by no particular reason. I have a horror of making excuses, and nothing I might say would serve to comfort her. My silence will allow her to formulate her own explanations: I have died, I have gone off the deep end, I have lost my memory, I have gone into seclusion. . . . In any case, she won't be the cause of my disappearance.

***

I return to my work, obliterating my name from the files of banks, ministries, department stores, magazines, newspapers, clubs, associations, political parties....Then I fabricate a new identity for myself: Marc Frechette, born in Venice, graduate of the San Diego Police School, resident of LA, holder of a driver's permit and a private detective's license. Upon reaching my destination, all I'll have to do is declare the loss of my identity cards for the American authorities to provide me with new, false, perfectly authentic ones.

I have decided to call myself Marc Frechette because I have discovered that I bear a striking resemblance to an actor of that name, the man who played the leading role in Antonioni's film *Zabriskie Point*. I love that film. I love old films. Frechette was working as a technician when he was discovered by representatives of Universal Studios: he was reproaching a man who had thrown a pot of geraniums at a couple quarreling in a bus station. During the shooting of the film, he didn't once cease criticizing Antonioni: he wanted the film to convey a pacifist message. Later, he joined a commune with his costar, Daria Halprin. Outraged by the revelations of Watergate, he held up a bank in Boston. One of his accomplices was shot by the police at the scene of the crime. Frechette was sentenced to twenty years in prison. When asked why he had robbed a bank, he replied:

"My act was intended as a political gesture. I watched the Watergate investigations on TV. I heard the Attorney General lie and John Dean tell the truth. I saw people lapsing more and more into apathy, and I felt an intense inner rage. They didn't know the truth, they didn't want to know it. But we knew it, and so we decided to show them. Because the banks are insured by the federal government, robbing them is a way of robbing Richard Nixon without doing anyone any harm. And, besides, I can think of no more honest act than aiming a gun at a teller emptying a safe."

In prison, Frechette staged a dramatization of Nixon's tapes. He was planning to take the production on a tour of the penitentiaries of the USA, when he was killed in 1975. He was found one morning in the gymnasium of Norfolk Prison, a 500-pound dumbbell lying across his neck. His death was pronounced accidental. He was buried in the cemetery at Forest Lawn.

***

When I step out of the Centre, the night lays its icy palms over my eyes. I have never seen myself in a mirror, never seen a photograph of myself. I have no voice, no history. The world does not exist between my ears. The world rests on a misunderstanding. I recall a dead sheep I once saw at the foot of a waterfall: the flesh had been stripped from the animal by the water and by marauding insects, leaving only the downy wool fluttering from the bones. It looked like the carcass of an angel.

Farewell, dear homeland. Sleep on, stay as you are, a people of no passion and no destiny. When my ancestors disembarked on these shores during the reign of Louis XIII, they wanted only one thing: to return forthwith to their homeland. But they had no money for the return voyage. Now, I am about to fulfill their ancient desire. The gusting wind has blown the snow into deep ridges, like the surface of a choppy lake. The bus that carries me to the airport trembles and shakes, while the trees outside the window bend low. But this cold is not so very severe. To attain the total repose of all matter, my laboratory would have to be removed from all external influences, from all outside interference. I conducted my research by night, when the streets were all but deserted. As you approach absolute zero, matter either crystallizes or superfluidifies. After the extinction of the last sun, the universe will resemble a snowflake.

LA

The neon lights in the airport terminal are reflected in the gray tile floor, which is streaked with soapy water. I sit before a TV screen and watch Susan Hayward submit to the caresses of John Wayne, playing the role of Genghis Khan. Stretched out on a sand dune, her arms raised above her head, she writhes seductively, her lovely face already assailed by invisible particles of plutonium. When she made this film in Utah, in 1954, the prevailing winds had carried toxic clouds into the area, the result of an atomic blast in Nevada the year before. The desert in which these actors worked was radioactive. Later, Wayne, Hayward, Pedro Armendariz and Agnes Moorehead would all die of cancer. Following the epilogue of *The Conqueror*, which I've just seen for the fifth time, I move to departure gate four. The moment I board the plane everything takes on a taste of plastic. When I disembark from the Boeing, I'm wearing a cowboy hat I bought in Chicago. Through the ramp window, I see the jet engines glittering in the LA sun. Thirty-odd passengers move toward the exit.

A taxi carries me to the Holiday Inn, where the Centre has reserved a room for me, all expenses paid, for a week: the best surprise is no surprise.

***

Today Marc Frechette, private detective, is officially open for business. In vain do I gaze at myself in the mirror. I can't get used to seeing myself with carrot-colored hair.

Thanks to my permit to carry a gun, obtained at the same time as a number of other cards issued in Frechette's name, I was able to purchase a .45, which I wear in a holster concealed beneath my jacket. While waiting for the ad in the LA *Times* to bring the desired results, I busy myself studying information on detection that I downloaded from an online police school website. From that site I also printed out a diploma bearing my name in large Gothic letters.

***

While tailing a suspect, a detective must take into account, not only the quality of the light on the street but also the intensity of the traffic....A detective is subject to long, unforeseeable absences: his assistants must be trained to cope with any sudden emergency....Instructions are usually conveyed by discreet, prearranged signals: change posts, stop, danger, increase surveillance....A detective surveying the movements of a suspect in a bar must take care to regulate his consumption of alcohol, so as to avoid any slipup at the moment of departure; in no event, must he let himself be taken in....Wall mirrors, rearview mirrors, store windows, all allow for surveillance as discreet as it is efficacious....Among those who, because of some form of mental derangement, are predisposed to crime, mention should be made of: mystical or systematic ecstatics, epileptics, degenerates, fanatics, hysterics, general paralytics, systematic psychotics, infectious toxic psychotics.

The actions of such individuals are not always characterized, however, by awkwardness, irrationality or impulsiveness. On the contrary, there is often nothing to betray the morbid nature of a criminal act.

***

I interrupt my studies briefly to take a walk in the park. At one point, I pick up a cat, pushing its paws away from my face, knowing that the eyeball has the consistency of a hard-boiled egg.

Solving an imaginary murder requires more than a little perspicacity, for the victim has been eliminated without the intervention of any physical act, but with very radical effects, his annihilation being complete, even in the memories he might have left behind him. As for a fictitious suicide, this touches upon the highest degree of complexity: anyone can shoot himself in the head—how could anyone miss such a close target?—but to liquidate himself, totally and irrevocably, demands the utmost intelligence, a mental astuteness often deemed by the uninformed to be madness or schizophrenia. It's like trying to remember an act you didn't commit.

I'm as busy as a bee, I don't stop for a moment. Between readings, I do push-ups, watch my biceps grow, probe my sore gum with my tongue, sit on the toilet and observe the second hand of my watch complete its circuit, stiffen when I hear what may be the footsteps of a prospective client in the hallway, yawn, indulge in a little introspection, try to feel what is called a sensation of universal love, recall old films I've seen, wonder how many thoughts unfold in my head in one day, count the hours that have passed since my arrival in this office, since I left Joelle.

It's been five days since I last saw my wife, whom I try to put out of mind by immersing myself in my new identity and attempting to lose all traces of my French accent. It's exactly as if she were dead. No news reaches me from the other side of the grave. I dreamed that she said to me: "I'm not going to die. I'm just going to step out of my body for a while. We all do that, constantly."

I must learn to act without thinking. I shall be near her only when I accept her death in my veins. I recall the first look we ever exchanged: nothing could disturb the intense, cool peace that encompassed those two little stars engaged in mutual contemplation.

***

I really have no idea where I'm going. My future I leave in the hands of fate. The dim light in this place is as much an impediment to truth as to falsehood. I must be patient, must ignore the countless voices trying to drown out the sense dispelled by the void. My eyes fill with tears. I clear my throat and spit a gob of bloodstained saliva into the wastebasket; it rolls off a wad of crumpled paper. More tears: this time I can't restrain them. My thoughts are so low. But I do what I can. I don't invent words; I seize them on the wing.

Once again, the great solar furnace has been ignited. The air conditioner emits its currents of cool air and its sepulchral rumblings. In the breath that passes behind the enclosure of the teeth, the entire universe breathes in, breathes out. Or stagnates. My memory is stifled, refusing to yield up the words my mother used to sing in my ear.

It's a matter of following an act right through to its end, once and for all. Highly hazardous highway, labyrinthine byway. Whether I'm tapping my fingers or my toes, I'm dancing. Or fidgeting. It all depends. The wave doesn't move in to the shore, it recedes. The respiration swells to the precise point of embracing its unfurling. Does anyone know at what level of dissimulation thought reigns? Lacking which, there is total collapse.

Like going too low or too high. A loss of. . . again that shadow, alternating between the letters and the page. Three lions gaze at themselves in a mirror at the back of the cage, slowly masticating the remains of their narcissistic trainer. The bricks of the house across the way absorb daylight like a sponge, then regurgitate a red froth all night.

***

Signs in porn-shop windows announce the most titillating books and magazines in the world. I find myself with a prostitute: *work it yourself, sweetie, yeah, that's the way, now come in me.* As I penetrate her, she pinches my nipples with the tips of her nails, causing me to ejaculate at once. And she wormed an extra twenty bucks out of me with a promise to prolong the pleasure. I hasten back to my apartment to take a shower, afraid I may have caught something I feel capable of killing. Instead of continuing along Sunset Boulevard, I climb the quiet streets of Beverly Hills. Her name was Lorene, she was fat and had the flushed face of an alcoholic. She appeared out of nowhere, at the very moment thoughts of Joelle had given me an erection.

I can't stand to be touched. Even the simple contact of the air against my skin galls me. In the park, several men are drinking from a bottle wrapped in a brown paper bag. I wonder how long it will be before I join their ranks. I've gone through most of my savings, no one has set foot in my office, and since I'm a stranger in this country I can't collect social welfare. Perhaps I'll end up staggering about the streets, bent double, trembling like a mutilated insect.

THE TOLL STATION

The highway begins just beyond the building, exploding in a million asphalted directions, all defiled, caressed, brutalized by countless automobile tires. It follows the curve of the earth over the entire continent, carrying police cars with their glitter domes, tractor-trailers with their diesel exhaust pipes, family sedans packed with children, motorcycles running in packs like wolves. I fill up my tank at a gas station with strings of little multicolored plastic flags, and then continue on my way, passing between giant billboards forbidding access to pedestrians, regulating weight, speed, direction, proclaiming the names of the towns I pass through. At one point, a barricade surrounded by large luminous arrows prevents access to a lane, where a work crew labors beneath the watchful gaze of two flag-waving robots, one to slow oncoming traffic, the other to send it blithely on its way. The rain dilutes the pools of gas and animal blood on the roadway and washes the crushed insects from my windshield. Like a spider setting foot on a thread of its own web, I sense beneath my Goodyear tires the reverberation of the billions of events taking place at this moment all along this interminable route, in Houston, New York, Vancouver, Montreal, all the places where we live, accelerate, brake, die. A divine road that weaves my destiny with its tiers of viaducts, its figure eights, its cloverleaves, its mind-boggling intersections.

From Sunset Boulevard to Sherbrooke Street, not a single interruption. I press the accelerator to the floor: no further need of brakes when the turnpike takes possession of my soul, temporarily putting an end to all my anguish. Tossing together all the disparate matter scattered over its surface, steel, concrete, rubber, flesh, it provides for our listening pleasure the incomparable sound of innumerable engines and their Doppler effect.

***

My first client is the manager of a toll station on the highway heading to Frisco. From the window of his office, he can observe the continual flow of vehicles in both directions, slowing only long enough to allow each driver to toss a coin into one of the little mesh baskets provided for that purpose on islets of concrete. Four employees in glass booths make change. A police car and a tow truck are stationed near the little air-conditioned cubicle, which is assailed day and night by noise, vibration and blasts of carbon monoxide. Mr. Kelp points to the tulips sitting in a can on his desk.

"They're plastic," he says, blowing his nose vigorously. "Nothing grows here. . . . But enough idle talk. My wife has disappeared. Can you find her for me?"

Once the question of the fee is settled, I ask Kelp what information he can give me to aid in my search.

"I think she's holed up at her brother's place in LA. His name is Harry Compton. He swears he hasn't seen her, but I don't believe him. I want you to go down there and check it out. If you find her, bring her back to me."

I explain to Kelp that I cannot force Carly to return. He gives me a suspicious look. To his query about my accent, I reply that I am from Texas.

"So, you're a blooming cowboy! Well, you just tell yourself that my wife is about to be eaten alive by a pack of coyotes in LA if she doesn't make quick tracks back to the ranch."

"I'll do my best to persuade her," I say, rising.

He accompanies me back to my car. I have made a note of the brother-in-law's address and slipped a photo of Carly with her pretty, frightened face into my jacket pocket. Kelp squeezes my elbow. "She has everything she could ask for here, you see? Listen, if you don't find her at Harry's, give me a buzz and we'll call the whole thing off. Because she could have beat it with any one of these bastards!" And he sweeps his arm through the air, taking in the hundreds of cars passing the station in an indescribable tumult of roaring engines and tossed coins.

"I call this the canyon of death," he says. "On each side you have eight high-speed lanes, with a narrow strip of concrete at the curb in case of an emergency. Every week, some idiot decides not to wait for the tow truck and gets out of his car to change a tire. And slam! He's pulled into the oncoming traffic, just like meat into a grinder. His body's found in little chunks spread out all over the highway. Sometimes they don't find the body at all, only the abandoned car and a few pools of blood."

***

Halfway to LA, as I begin to play my collection of Rolling Stones CDs for the sixth time, I leave the highway and take the road to Tecopa, Amargosa and Death Valley. The Mojave Desert seems to have stepped right out of a western film, with its red peaks, its giant green cactus, its molten sky. Just this side of the Nevada border, in a valley almost devoid of vegetation, I spot what I'm looking for: a sign announcing a piece of land for sale. I shut off the motor and walk toward the only habitation in sight, a ramshackle shed constructed of billboards, bricks and cellophane paper. I pick my way through a wilderness of hens, old tires and boards bristling with rusty nails, and from an artesian well pump a little water and sprinkle it over my face. The little muddy pool in which for a moment I can make out my reflection evaporates almost at once in the sun. I call. No reply. I enter the shack. On the table are two stale doughnuts and an empty beer bottle. Spotting a thin mattress on the floor, I decide to get a few hours' sleep.

I am awakened by the sounds of barking. I rise and go outside and am met by the spectacle of a dog with one blue eye and one black eye snapping at the haunches of a sheep caught in a thicket. Seated on a rock, an old cowboy is quietly drinking a cup of coffee. I proffer my package of cigarettes and he gestures me forward. Suddenly, I hear a low, snarling sound, like the distant roar of a motorcycle.

"My son," the man says simply.

I shift my gaze toward the granite peaks, which

are almost black in the blinding sunlight. In this heat, things vibrate and dissolve and momentarily lose all perspective.

"How much do you want for this land?"

"What you want it for?"

"Nothing in particular."

The man nods, as if this was the only reasonable answer to his question, and names a price. I bargain a little, for the sake of it. Very quickly, we come to an agreement. I make an appointment to meet him a month hence in the land registry office in Tecopa, where the transaction will be finalized. Then I continue on my way to LA, accompanied behind the hills by a cloud of dust raised by the invisible son on his motorcycle.

***

Harry, the brother-in-law, lives in a split-level house with an enormous chimney rising up in the middle. When I arrive, the driveway is obstructed by a motorboat on a trailer and a small house-trailer. The lawn is green concrete. From the backyard come the sounds of merriment, shouts and laughter and strains of rock music. I circle the house and join the party. About a dozen adults are hacking at pieces of grilled chicken with plastic utensils and drinking beer from big paper cups. The hostess welcomes me with a smile: have a seat, have something to eat. I mutely comply. The talk is of football. I ask a pretty brunette where I can find Carly.

"I haven't the slightest idea," she says with a laugh. "I don't know a soul here myself. But Harry can probably tell you."

She adds that, as usual, our host has taken refuge in the basement, that I can't possibly miss him. I make my way through the kitchen: plates, pots, empty 7-Up cans, torn potato-chip bags are piled in the sink, over which hangs the inevitable wall clock. On the wall next to the window is a stuffed Snoopy doll.

I descend the staircase to the basement. Behind a bar, illuminated by a lamp whose globe bears the inscription "Genius at Work," a bald man with a pointed chin, wearing a white shirt with snap-fastener buttons and black cotton pants, is preparing a cocktail for a fat woman with varicose veins.

"Harry?" I ask.

He raises his glass. "That's me. My hobby is drinking. I enjoy nothing better on weekends than entertaining my friends and getting myself plastered."

"I'm looking for Carly."

"Why, you want to screw her?"

With only a trace of unsteadiness, he steps up to me and exhales his foul breath in my face, while, in the depths of a velvet armchair, the fat lady sits sipping her drink. I hesitate, before replying with a wink:

"That's right, I want to fuck your sister."

He slaps his thigh, impressed by my frankness.

"I got Carly a job as an usherette at Anaheim Stadium. She won't be back before eleven. Take a seat, tell me all about yourself."

The Ascent

I drive at random through the streets of LA in my rented Chevrolet. In an attempt to banish my pain and fear, I stop at Dino's Bar, order a whisky and ask for a ticket to tonight's hockey game. The barman sells me a seat at an exorbitant price.

Nocturne. The city stretches along the seashore. A heavy rain transforms the streets into dark mirrors, in which the skyscrapers are dimly reflected. The arches of the elevated highway disappear into the smog. The wind whistles faintly about the buildings. Empty buses move toward the terminal. The traffic lights on Sunset Boulevard stretch into the distance, vanishing in the mist. The neon signs of amusement arcades wink on and off in the deserted night. The city exists by virtue of a mysterious mathematics. The rain falls on the homes of the stars in Beverly Hills, on San Bernardino Park with its lofty palms and its empty picnic tables, on the skyscrapers clustered near the seashore, on the suburbs to the east and the north, on Anaheim Stadium.

The gigantic circular structure with its Doric columns and its corrugated cornice looks as if it might at any moment begin spinning, like a casino roulette. The parking lot stretching all about it resembles a frozen black lake with yellow and white lines painted on it. Before the matches, the spectators flock here to eat hot dogs.

The players step onto the ice. I live each of their movements vicariously. I skate, swerve, shoulder my way through the defense, given up to a purely kinetic monologue that projects me into the illusory space of the game. Violently illuminated by spotlights, the ice has the intense luminosity of the sacred host at the moment of transubstantiation. This is my body. In fact, I occupy a dozen bodies, angelic and demonic. I carry the puck on the blade of my stick, I elude an adversary, 18,000 mouths open simultaneously to cheer me on, I no longer belong to myself. I shoot. Propelled at a speed that renders it invisible to the naked eye, though it will be picked up on the slow-motion TV screen, the rubber disk strikes the goaltender's plastic mask just above the eye.

I wait in vain for the face-off. I raise my eyes. I'm all alone on the ice. I look to see if there are any spectators left in the stands. I can't move. From the cold in my limbs, I realize that I am under the ice, frozen stiff. Then the puck drops in front of me, shaking me out of my torpor. But it's too late: I've lost the face-off.

A wave of incredulous surprise is emitted by the brain whenever it is asked to react to something incongruous or absurd, reflecting the effort required to lend meaning to that which has none. It sweeps through me, as I try desperately to find an explanation for my presence here in the stands. An usherette in a red tunic with gold epaulets smiles at me: I recognize Carly.

***

After the match, hundreds of neon lights begin to hum in unison. Once empty, this monumental place seems strangely miniscule.

"They said you wanted to see me?" she asks, emerging from one of the tunnels. I can see her reflection in the plate-glass partition above the gate, a bronze silhouette in a bikini top and shorts, standing against the white backdrop of the rink.

"Can I buy you a drink?"

French? she asks. I shake my head: no, I'm from Quebec. Standing with one hip thrown slightly out, she plays with a gold serpent entwined about her right arm just below the elbow. A person could easily get lost in this large circular structure where everything looks the same, I tell her. She points to the exit, stepping around a beer cart that two attendants are pushing toward an elevator. She says she's crazy about hockey, especially during the play-offs, when the teams are often obliged to play what she calls a period of "sudden death" overtime.

At centre-ice, near the face-off circle, painters are using a plywood frame to spray the home team's emblem on the ice: a green crown. A voice announces over the loudspeakers: "One, two, three. . . testing, one, two, three. . .," the words echoing loudly beneath the huge dome. A camera attached to a long metal arm is focused directly on us. A giant black cube high above centre-ice holds a digital dock, used to indicate the amount of time remaining in each period; the numbers have just clicked back to zero.

We gaze at the myriad lights of LA twinkling beyond the stadium windows. The painters nod to us as they pass. I want to move inside the orbit of her clothing, to cover her footprints with my own, to navigate all the way to her blond hair, then to lay her beneath me and enter her. I try to imagine her bare back on a Santa Monica beach, recalling a prayer I read somewhere: "Dear Lord, guide us safely to death."

***

46

I lead her to the back of the bar, to a cubicle containing only one bench, obliging her to sit beside me squeezed against the wall. As I reach for the menu, my forearm grazes her breast. The TV screen above the bar shows a shot of the Great Wall of China: a solitary spruce tree trembles beneath the ramparts, a green triangle caressed by the wind. She says she misses the trees of Rochester, her home town. I make an effort to reply, to produce those little things, what do they call them?

Words? Yes, that's it, words! She says she's only working temporarily as an usherette, awaiting a chance to get into movies.

I ask her how she manages to express the feelings of others. She says all actors are liars. I tell her of two films I long to see: the first, a simple carpet, examined with a macroscopic lens, transformed gradually into a strange planet populated with unknown plants and animals; the second depicting at a greatly accelerated pace the entire life of a character, who would actually grow before the viewer's eyes, moving across a rapid succession of landscapes, as day succeeds night, and night day, until finally he dies, his body decomposing with explosive speed.

She tells me she's dating the goaltender of the local

hockey team, who is away on tour on the east coast. She has the use of his Santa Monica villa for a week. Why don't we make use of it together? We can spend our days on the beach. I tell her I'll think about it. You're married, she says, I can tell that right away. She raises one hand to touch my forehead. I draw back. Scared? she asks. I'm only trying to be nice. She finds me cold, hostile. But she'll change me, bring me out of my shell.

I tell her I've abandoned my family. Desertion, they call it. But my wife has enough to live on. She writes advertisements for naturalist magazines and McDonald's restaurants. The children have their TV set and their mother. They'll hate me, and forget me. As for myself, I feel nothing. As long as I don't run out of money, I'll probably remain in this semi-stupor. Every dollar buys a few moments of oblivion. If I were rich, I would already have forged a new lifestyle for myself. Remorse is a sentiment of the poor. When my resources are depleted, I'll return and make my excuses. Nervous breakdown, they'll say.

She asks me if I think I'm capable of loving another person. Listen, I tell her, they can attach electrodes to your head and tell whether or not you will like a certain product. They don't even ask your opinion: you might lie, unconsciously, and for any number of reasons. "So if you really want to know if I'm capable of loving," I say, "you'll have to send me to the Neurocommunications Clinic at Harvard. But I'm broke."

She presses herself up against me and says: "I hope you don't believe all that nonsense."

Back outside, we stand beneath the awning of a candy shop, clinging to each other. Time stops. I caress her cautiously: every stray hair, hardened by the chronological trance, is as sharp as a razor. I am no longer able to measure my movements by the revolutions of the sun. In the absence of any foreseeable future, my thoughts grow sparse. Words form so slowly in my brain that I lose track of their sequence. It takes me an eternity to tell her I love her. I press my brow to hers: her eyes converge, become a hazy sun at the zenith of a world of eyebrows and flesh.

I can't believe that I'm going to forget all this: this street, this body, this moment. How do things disappear? Releasing herself from my embrace, Carly shows me the footprint of Rita Hayworth embedded in a bronze plaque in the sidewalk.

"See how small it was! They say she sometimes appeared to passers-by, her lips moving silently, as if she wanted to tell them that none of this really exists. I think she was searching for the movie sets she once worked on."

We cross the boulevard to a square containing a solitary tree, a picnic table and a bench, on which a bum lies, curled up. At the back of the square is a blind brick wall, on which is painted a forest with palm trees and spruce trees and a pond whose gray water merges with the gravel in the square.

I bend over the vagabond and shout in his ear: "Are you all right? Are you happy here in your forest?"

The man awakens with a start and rolls to the ground. Scrambling to his feet, he brushes stones from his brown jacket and baggy pants and mutters: "Goddamnit, leave me alone!"

The combined effects of sunshine, fresh air and alcohol have lent the man's face a dry, coppery texture, as if a single coat of paint had been applied to the bones and cartilage. His bloodshot eyes dart anxiously about in their sockets.

"Are you happy?"

He trembles with rage and cold. He glances nervously about, as if seeking assistance, then makes a move to depart. I seize him by the wrist.

"Let him go," says Carly.

We walk in silence for several minutes. I wasn't trying to make fun of him, I tell her, I simply wanted to know how he survives. I was even ready to give him a little money. You looked as if you wanted to kill him, she replies.

***

We enter a discotheque, where a black man invites Carly to dance. Studiously sucking the olive from my martini, I recall the cave on Patmos where Saint John is reputed to have written the Apocalypse. The guide indicated the fissure in the rock through which the evangelist heard the voice of God. I should have stayed there until the miracle was repeated. Instead of which, here I am, sitting in a dark club, listening to the loudspeaker multiply the decibels of Jim Morrison's "Light my Fire," a song written and sung by a man who died of alcohol abuse and whose body is buried in Père-Lachaise but whose voice continues to cry: "Papa, I want to kill you, Mama, I want to…"

The dance ends. Carly takes the half-empty bottle of beer her partner hands her and drains it in a single gulp, while the customers applaud. A shower of sweat has plastered her hair to her skull. Her breasts heave as she gasps for air. Then the uproar resumes. She closes her eyes, raising her arms to the ceiling, where a complicated network of neon lights flash on and off, on and off, each time depicting a different animal: butterfly, gazelle, leopard. . . .The ecstatic grimaces of drunken couples etch strange hieroglyphics in the air, like those Mayan bas-reliefs depicting a cortege of demons. A strobe light dismembers the movements of my fingers as they scoop salted peanuts from a baked clay dish.

I rush for the exit. Outside, the rain falls softly on my black leather jacket while the roar of a jet plane fades into the distance, its twin lights receding northward in the direction of the Canadian border. I decide to leave Carly here. She excites me too much. What if I should lose control of myself? I banish the image of a knife sinking slowly between two small conical breasts. The tires of the car squeal on the wet pavement. Now, I'm climbing the hill leading to the municipal aqueduct.

***

But Carly is beside me. She reaches out and takes my hand. LA seems to have been born of the infinite geometric projection of a single square. Except no one knows the rules that govern the movements of the pawns on this enormous chessboard; they are shunted about at will, following Euclidian lines that stretch into spaces that are purely imaginary.

In my room at the Holiday Inn, I kneel before her and remove the vinyl boots she put on in the discotheque. She wriggles her toes, then removes a chocolate bar from her purse and bites off a piece. Beneath our window, a militant feminist is distributing pamphlets to passers-by, surrounded by heaps of discarded papers, torn, rumpled, marked by footprints, splattered with ice cream, sniffed at by dogs, the poor-quality ink running in the rain until the text is obscured. I close the curtains.

Carly is seated on the bed in my bathrobe, her legs tucked beneath her. On the radio, a seemingly endless progression of sounds synthesized by a computer follows a trajectory that appears to be purely whimsical but which, in fact, conforms to a strict pattern of logarithms. I give myself up to the body stretched beneath me, to its warm, malleable surfaces, crossing the frontier to a world which, despite its strangeness, remains friendly, for it too is promised to the void. I try to melt into it. Failing to comprehend life, we can always neutralize it. Sometimes, however, my thoughts run in the opposite direction. Then sea and sky become thin, transparent films hanging before a fluid, dark mass that is at once intangible, incalculable, imperceptible. I shudder with joy at the promise of death. I take note of each modification of my present state. Thanks to my heightened awareness, the differences are multiplied, accelerated. I smile as I find myself drawn into an ever expanding space that has no name and no coordinates. Now, I'm swept up in a marvelous dance

Must keep going. Mustn't stop. Coming and going, in waves, like the act of love making itself. I slow down or accelerate, according to the intensity of the pleasure. I draw the hair away from her ear and, pulling gently on the pierced lobe, whisper to her, my eyes fixed on the orifice, the sinuous curves of the flesh, the hole into which the words drop, one by one, causing the eardrum to vibrate, setting up a number of unpredictable detonations between the neurons, a sort of gasping effect, a muscular undulation. I say just anything that comes into my head, and we both laugh at such unbridled license. Crystals arranged helter-skelter in my throat vibrate and sing with the passage of each breath.

***

Now, no one can tear me from the dream that runs through my veins. I amuse myself in observing my consciousness hover lazily about me, weaving its way about my indistinct and ever changing surroundings. I hear Carly slam the bathroom door. She seems alarmed, angry. She stretches out at my side. I make no effort to banish the image of her in the white dress of sacrifice, her hands bound behind her back. The wind has risen and the waves are crashing on the shore. From time to time, the headlights of a car pass behind the dunes. She challenges me with a look. I tear the veil. Later, we lie quietly side by side. I try in vain to hear the beating of her heart: it is drowned out by the ocean's roar.

The night has many voices. The marvel of prophecy. The key to the future lies in our dreams. I give my senses full rein. Words come in reverse order and set things straight. Their entry onto the scene provokes much laughter and applause. They make a tour of the track, then depart, unseen, unknown. Oh, the cruelty of Aeneas abandoning Dido in Carthage! Now, my freedom is restricted by the advent of images, whose pressure I feel throughout my entire body, like a diver sinking into the watery depths. Now, the internal transmitters announce only catastrophes, flesh quakesvolcanoes that fizzle out beneath the inoperative brain. Never again will I allow myself to become trapped in a life that offers nothing but the empty form of routine. I cannot retrace my steps. I move deeper and deeper into the labyrinth, knowing all the while that I am the shortest distance from one point to the next. The knife pierces the breast so gently that it takes several minutes to reach the heart.

The conflagrations of thought momentarily illuminate the flowers of pale pink paper, causing me to groan, my brow furrowed, my eyelids twitching: incomplete outward manifestations of the dream. When I awaken, I won't remember the countless illusions that have articulated my sleep. On the roof of a building, I juggle daggers, while two big, dangerous dogs prowl about the countryside below. Then Carly subjects me to a strange intelligence test: first, I must slide a number of steel disks into a transparent tube; then, I must cut a spinning top into very thin slices and shuffle them like playing cards. I'm curious to know whether I'm not struggling with a problem that is, in fact, insoluble. I decide to leave this small, inhospitable town. I call the station for information: there are bus lines in all directions across the wild, mountainous countryside. I rent a bi-plane. Flying over the desert, I spot a number of armored cars down below, awaiting the signal to attack. Suddenly, tracer bullets climb in my direction.

***

In the morning, I inform Carly that I am a detective.

"In fact, I have been retained by your husband."

"So you have nothing better to do with your time than track down women who've run away from their husbands?"

Very quickly, I attain a level of total objectivity: Carly's body suddenly loses all its appeal, it occupies a certain space, that's all, composed of matter as inert and indifferent as the table at which I sit.

Nothing can touch me now. It is Marc Frechette who suffers and fears, who gulps down four aspirins to combat a migraine that is like a metal band clamped about his skull. Clearly, this poor detective is on the verge of madness. In the grip of such sorrow, what can I do? All I want is to achieve a state of oblivion. But who is in charge here? Who is thinking in this strange language, in this strange time and place? My God, I wish I were under a hundred feet of water!

Somehow, I must regain access to myself. I proceed as I used to when searching the memory of the computer for some nonintegrated fact, taking careful inventory of the objects and qualities that make up the semantic field. But this operation demands a number of properties I no longer possess: am I hot, white, desperate, wet, detective or programmer, living or dead?

The words won't come to help me organize my thoughts; it's as if I were suspended in some intermediary state, somewhere beyond their definitions.

"How much did Kelp offer you to bring me back?'

"An extra thousand."

"So I'll tell you what we do: I'll go back with you and you split the thousand with me."

''And, the next day, you'll be gone again?"

"That's right. I'll meet you at the goaltender's place."

"All right, it's a deal."

We stop for a few moments at Harry's place, where several couples are frolicking in the pool, the women mounted on the men's backs trying to knock one another into the water, where they splash about and guzzle beer. The sun spins like a silver coin in the LA sky: heads or tails? Red or black? Odds or evens? Carly returns with a suitcase. I set it on the back seat and we leave the city.

Three hours later, I turn her over to Kelp. He hands me ten $100 bills. Carly already has my check for $500 in her purse.

SANTA MONICA

The next morning, I awaken to the joyful prospect of rejoining Carly in Santa Monica. I dress, pack my bag and am on my way out the door when a thought suddenly strikes me: it's there. I don't know what it is, because it's constantly changing, altering shapes, masks, disguises. But it's there, waiting for me, silent, impassive, never increasing or decreasing in size, absolutely indifferent to anything I might say or do or think. Though I try repeatedly to seize it, subjugate it, destroy it, magnify it, I know I shall never succeed. Breaking into laughter, I strike the wall with my fist and repeat in a loud voice: "It's there."

And it seems to me that, in so saying, I have spoken the last word on the subject, that any further discourse or reflection will be superfluous. Sinking to my knees on the floor, I press my hands and face to the floorboards, as happy as a lost child who has found its mother.

It strikes me that behind the words there may be an entire universe, one which has absolutely no duration, which is here one moment and gone the next. I try to imagine something literally passing through my head, in one side and out the other. But nothing can occupy the same space as my brain; nothing but my consciousness, that is, which is all pervasive. There is a lot of smog this morning in this gray-and-white city, the movie-television capital of the world. All this started partly with the invention of the Kodak camera by George Eastman, gay sportsman who took his own life in the belief that he was taking the ultimate photo. To his heirs he bequeathed the grand sum of $350,000,000 and a chateau that was transformed into a museum. In 1897, he had the world's first electric sign installed in Trafalgar Square, with the following words emblazoned on it:

You Pull The Switch

We Do The Rest

He also invented the word *Kodak*.

"I considered a great number of combinations, all beginning and ending with my favorite letter, *K*, such a strong, peremptory letter! The word *Kodak* was the result of all my research." On an African safari, Eastman filmed a charging rhinoceros. The hunter accompanying him shot the beast when it was only fifteen paces from his master; it dropped to the ground two paces from Eastman. When reproached for unnecessarily risking his life, Eastman replied: "One must always have confidence in the members of one's organization."

Before shooting himself through the heart, he left a note between two bars of soap on the edge of the bathtub: "My usefulness is past. It would be pointless to go on." The official biographies published by Kodak make no mention of this suicide, which caused the company's fortunes to founder temporarily in 1932.

***

It enrages me to think of the little money left to me. I've gone through almost all my savings. I'll have to rely on my credit cards, which may soon be revoked. I switch off the lights and go down to the front desk, where I instruct them to send my bill to the Centre. Emerging from the building, I sense for the first time that I am on alien soil. I stand on the wind-swept terrace, facing the sea, the sun beating down on me. Soon, it will begin to cool. A faint luminous halo, in appearance beneficent, fills the sky, like millions of sparks blown into the atmosphere from the earth's fiery center through an imaginary hole in its crust. Sometimes, it seems to me that all things are one, infinitely large or infinitely small, depending on my vantage point, and that I am part of them, that we are all rolling blindly in space. Of course, we don't "roll," but in attempting to find the word I am looking for, I realize to what point it is impossible to say what I want to say.

I ask the doorman to bring my car around to the front of the building. I must remain in control, even at the cost of my life. I bite my lip to prevent myself from smiling: I don't want the Japanese tourists to take me for a lunatic. My flight must be methodical, my psychic energy concentrated somewhere in the back of my throat, at that point at which the alchemy of the breath and the nerves takes place. Because, ahead of me, I see nothing. The possibilities seem infinite, but when the sense of the whole thing becomes clear, the innovations prove in fact to be of a minor order. So often that is the case, the role played by chance in our lives being very small, if not negligible. This time, I can't restrain my laughter. The doorman gives me a sharp look, shrugging as he pockets his tip. How could I possibly explain it? I would only risk betraying myself. Better to hold my tongue. I must nourish the fear, for it alone is real. The drunks muttering to themselves beneath the pilings down by the seashore know what I mean.

My organs escape me. I am multiplied from head to toe, according to an infinite variety of existential designs. I'm amused by my repeated failures to get a grip on my own totality. These very failures are milestones on the highway of my existence. I sneeze, as I invariably do when confronted with the sublime, realizing that I am lost. But this vague recollection doesn't help me to find my way. I enter a restaurant to ask for directions, but I can't understand the waitress with the pink ribbon in her hair. I decide to take a rest. A cup of coffee saturated with sugar revives the ache in a decaying tooth. My muscles are sore and my eyes are burning. I order a second cup of coffee. At the next table, a traveling salesman is explaining the advantages of latex over oil in the manufacture of paint. Imprinted on a shroud, what traces does reality leave? He was making a delivery when the customer suddenly opened a suitcase to reveal the plaster head of a Christ she had decapitated in a church. One application every four years is more than enough, and results in less blistering. Then the sky was rent in two, like a sheet of cheap wallpaper. All nature erupted in boils from the outrage perpetrated against the Almighty. We have a factory right here in LA, we guarantee delivery within 24 hours. I punch out a number on my cell phone, and hear a deep humming sound, like the sacred *om* of the Orient. Hello, how are you doing this morning? Yes, I checked out of the hotel a short while ago....She gives me instructions on how to reach the place. She'll probably be on the beach, but she'll leave the door unlocked.

A black Mustang, which I recall seeing upon entering the restaurant, pulls away behind me. I must be mistaken: no one would waste time tailing me through the streets of LA. Who could possibly be interested in my movements? The suspicion that I'm being followed can have no foundation in reality. On the winding road that follows the coast, the immense blue clamor of the Pacific on my left, the cliffs rising sheer on my right, I can see no one behind me, the route lies open in both directions.

It's there. I repeat the words, striking the steering wheel with my fist, laughing at the top of my lungs. Always there, always present, in the liquid or the solid or the gaseous state, in my blood, in my bones, in my breath....

I continue on my way, forcing myself to take the curves without diminishing speed. The tires squeal on the pavement, as my body is pressed up against the car door. The lavish villas of Santa Monica stand in stark profile against the moonlit sky. Now the circle is about to be squared, leaving me a perfect orb within the square of death. The house has a blue façade, with four square columns set into brick. The heat blurs the shapes of things. I ring the doorbell, then turn to face the street. I must look suspicious, leaning against the wall like this in my rumpled clothes. There is no answer. I open the door and enter. From somewhere nearby, I hear the rhythmic blasts of a car horn. A cat darts between my legs. A bicycle stands in the hallway, chained to a radiator. The wallpaper is peeling in places, revealing the dusty, gray slats beneath.

A shower, clean clothes, a can of peaches. I drink the syrup straight from the can, then lie down for a nap. When I awaken, Carly is standing before me, wearing a black silk dress and high-heel shoes. She has put on perfume and painted her lips and her eyelids. She approaches the bed. I run my hands over her, as the tears stream down my face. Little by little, the cold leaves me.

She sets two glasses of wine on the bedside table. Our love, she says, is incestuous and narcissistic: you, my brother... you, myself. . . like making love to one's own reflection. I smile. All my anguish suddenly leaves me. In the dimly lit room, with the curtains drawn, it is as if a star were speaking to me: you, who wait. . . you, the subject... She says nothing. Stranded over LA, a distant star casts its last pale rays upon us, like a faint murmur out of space. The signs are interchangeable. I want to remain forever in this house, from whose windows I can see the flickering beacon of the lighthouse and hear the pounding waves on the shore.

**

She opens the curtains to let the sunshine in. "Wake up, we're going to the beach. You can have your coffee down there." In the car, she sings softly: *I don't know no love song, I can't sing the blues anymore, but baby it's all right...*

The red Frisbee floats through the air filled with the pungent odors of picnickers' fires, banks into a curve near the parasol and drops toward the plastic tablecloth. Carly catches it, then stretches her bronzed body and sends it sailing back to me. It strikes the water at my feet with a loud plop! I sing a song by the Beach Boys.

"Tonight we'll come back with a fluorescent Frisbee," she says. "It's like playing with the moon."

I would love to run my hands over every inch of her lovely body. Sky and sea merge. Convinced for the moment that everything in the world is perfect, I pass in review before the half-clad bodies stretched out on beach towels. I step around the pink pool of a melted Popsicle, its two wooden sticks lying side by side in the sand. How should one experience such moments, punctuated by periods of test and agitation, waiting and oblivion, anxiety and reassurance? I lack the patience to achieve a state of articulated awareness extended through time. I prefer to seize the moments as they pass, as purely esthetic experiences. The entire planet photographed by the light of nuclear flashes. Don't forget to turn out the lights before you leave. The cold waves breaking against my legs, Carly's footprints in the sand, seagulls perched on the rims of garbage pails, kites stretching toward the surfers riding the waves....

***

We cross Wilshire Boulevard to a great clay pit that, millions of years ago, was the home of a multitude of animal species, all now extinct. A half-million specimens of tyrannosaurs and brontosaurs have been exhumed here, as well as prehistoric versions of mammals, lizards and birds. Leaning on the concrete balustrade, Carly informs me that the 5000-year-old skeleton of an Indian woman was found in this pit. All about the pitch-lined holes stand the menacing figures of life-size monsters on plastic feet. I slap her on the rump.

"Fool!"

"I'm a fool for you!"

Wandering aimlessly in the dusk. Eating oysters at a sidewalk concession. Let's eat, drink and be merry, my love, for we shall never die.

***

This afternoon, I'm alone. She's at work at the stadium. Standing straight, immobile, in my cage of flesh and bone, I gaze at the sky, hoping passers-by will be drawn to imitate me, taken in by the classic gag. I can't see anything except an occasional flash high in the stratosphere; perhaps it comes from some space laboratory. It seems at moments as if the entire field of my vision were an unidentified flying object, a UFO, which is about to transport me to another world where I will learn how to reverse time and to displace the planets.

I stop at a grocery store and buy a bottle of Chablis. Shirtless, my cowboy hat perched on the back of my head, I pass through a park, where a group of tourists is admiring a golden pagoda. I sense that I'm being observed: a nudge of the elbow, a pointed finger. Look, it's him! Do you think so? Yes, that's the hat he wore in his last western! Sir, could I have your autograph? They are seeing a man who died in 1975. In electronic time, all actors, all movies, all people exist simultaneously.

Without replying, I turn into the driveway of a sumptuous villa, whose owner is on almost permanent vacation. I stop and glance over my shoulder. The young woman who was following me hesitates at the gateway, then retraces her steps to the tour bus, drawn by the blasting of the horn, distressed at her failure to obtain the autograph of Marc Frechette. Smiling, I circle the house and push my way through a clump of bougainvillea, finding myself back at the cottage.

Branches trace a cursory, vegetal latticework against the LA sky. Shriveled camellias stand in little clumps of dry grass. For two weeks, water has been rationed, because up in the mountains there is not enough snow. In their calcified cloaks of dust, the trees seem to be slowly dissolving, like mirages in the desert.

The sausages sizzle in the frying pan, filling the kitchen with smoke. I open the balcony door. On the veranda of the neighboring house stands a camera, its lens pointed straight in my direction. There is a click: the camera must be set to function automatically, controlled by a mechanism that releases the shutter at spaced intervals, allowing the seemingly accelerated recording of a blooming flower or a setting sun. Standing behind the half-drawn curtains, I eat my lunch. Should I remain here for hours, my appearance at this window would appear on the video as no more than a fleeting apparition.

***

Constantly surveying their surroundings, their little heads darting to and fro, a number of birds hop about on the lawn. I throw breadcrumbs to the little tweeters, whose names I do not know and who awaken me each morning, while Carly goes on sleeping soundly at my side. I peer into the distance, trying to make out the sparkling waters of the Pacific, then shift my gaze slightly to focus on a shimmering cloud of carbon monoxide hanging over a seemingly endless stream of cars, their unpredictable, jerky movements like drops of mercury on a plate: a fitting backdrop for the bougainvillea bushes of our absentee neighbor.

California Express

Someone is at the door. I open it to discover the red-headed giant, Kelp. Behind him is the black Mustang I saw following me through the streets of LA. Speaking slowly and gravely, he asks me for a few minutes of my time. He precedes me into the living room, taking long, unhurried strides, like a military man out of uniform. He passes a hand with a missing index finger through his hair, the veins in his forearm bulging like cables. There is a look of almost violent serenity on his face. He lowers his bulk onto the sofa, among Carly's furs and silks and satins.

"You two pulled a fast one on me," he says simply. "The day after you brought Carly back, she was gone again. With my $500 bucks. When the clerk at the bank told me she'd cashed a big check, I put two and two together and decided to advance the date of my vacation a little and pay you both a visit. I like playing the detective. Now, I've got several photos to prove your adultery. And I also know you're not an American citizen and that this isn't your house. You've got forty-eight hours to come up with my thousand bucks, plus $3000 in damages and interest."

"And if I fail?"

"I'll turn you in. You're lucky your wife hasn't filed a complaint against you. There's a law against running out on your family, you know. And I'll lay charges of fraud against you. But I don't want to make things unnecessarily difficult for you. Pay me what you owe me and you won't spend the next three years behind bars. I prefer to settle things privately."

The unusually gentle quality of his voice lends his words a cadence that is almost musical. After a moment, he rises and begins to move about the room. Very calmly, he overturns the music stand and smashes the cello. He takes books from the shelves and methodically breaks their bindings. He's clearly enjoying himself. Then, as calm and relaxed as ever, he lowers himself into a leather armchair, takes a long Russian cigarette from a pack and, holding it between thumb and forefinger, lights it. The net curtains of the window filter the harsh sunlight. A strange peace settles over me, as if my very thoughts had acquired a substance that dissipates the threat even before it has a chance to take shape.

Kelp tells me we'll be seeing each other again in the near future, then rises to leave.

"In your place," he adds, "I'd get the hell out of here. I don't imagine the owner of this house will be very happy when he sees all this damage and when he learns you've been sleeping with his girl. By the way, you have no work permit and your credit cards have all been cancelled."

Then he takes his leave, tapping me amicably on the shoulder in passing.

I hasten to tidy up the place before Carly returns from the stadium. Kelp didn't do too much damage; he was just giving me a warning. He must have got the goaltender's address at the stadium. He's probably been surveying our comings and goings for days now, awaiting an opportunity to find me alone. I can't give him $4000. I don't have anywhere near that amount. What worries me is how far such an individual may be willing to go to get what he wants.

I hide the broken cello in a cupboard in the cellar, then take my .45 automatic from the plastic bag in which it is carefully wrapped. I remove the clip from the butt and check that there are ten cartridges in it, then, aiming at a pot of paint, pull back the hammer and squeeze the trigger. There is the dull snap of steel against steel. I pack my bag, concealing the weapon beneath a pile of clothes.

Carly returns with two tickets for a concert at the Hollywood Bowl. I suggest she go with a girlfriend. Hasn't in occurred to her that the owner of the villa might return a day early and find us together in bed? I prefer not to run such a risk, I'd rather get out while the going is good.

"You're right," she says. "Bob's a good man. I'll tell him I'm leaving him, as discreetly as possible."

She suggests a hotel in the center of the city. I hesitate a moment, realizing that I have scarcely a hundred dollars to my name. She promises to join me there as soon as she's laid the cards on the table.

"I broke Bob's cello," I tell her. "If he makes a fuss about in, I'll buy him a new one."

"All right, I'll reimburse you."

Before leaving, I take her in my arms and hold her a little too tightly. She makes me swear that I won't run out on her, that I'll wait for her. I replace the emblem on the hood of my Chevrolet and decide to stop at a car wash. After the squall of spray hoses, the assault of the vertical and horizontal roller-brushes, the timid jet of wax, the caress of the chamois cloths, the hurricane of the powerful ventilators, I pass a sign that reads:

Your Car Has Just Been Chemically Cleaned
By An Anti-Pollution Procedure

Thank You Come Again

The water evaporates from the body of the car as I head into LA on the eight-lane expressway. It's impossible to tell if anyone is following me, and for the moment I don't care.

***

The void is located inside and outside the world of appearances. Which leaves one free to turn in circles. But, for the moment, I don't want to think. To think is to set death squarely before yourself and then to make a choice. No one wants to think. I feel as if I were suffocating. I open the window of my hotel room and stick my head out. Two big teenage girls are barking like dogs at a policeman on a motorcycle. I feel as if I were in a station waiting for a train that will never come. It is reality itself that will depart promptly on time, leaving me stranded here on the platform, a suitcase in each hand; it will depart and never return.

A rattling sound rises in my throat, in which I recognize the faint rumblings of those enigmatic little things called words. Words take root in my body, and vice versa. I stick my thumb down the back of my throat and vomit on the tile floor in the bathroom.

My brain lies congealed inside a steel box. I put my faith in the savor of circumstances. I live in a state of lethargic content. For me, social existence is merely a palliative ordering of situations that, in themselves, are intolerable. Personal improvisations, the immense after-snows of spring, the intricate lacework of ever accelerating movements: these are what I have tried to learn. But now I must discover a way of dispelling my emotions before they take shape, for they have the capacity to destroy me. The world has exhausted all the possible combinations of passions. And I detest pleonasms.

I walk down the strip of grass in the center of the avenue, getting my shoes wet in the dew-soaked grass, inhaling the odors of gasoline, fried foods and burnt rubber. An orchestra in gold-trimmed uniforms plays in the bandstand, while policemen encircle the park with a chain link fence. Sometimes I think in English, amazed at how differently my thoughts emerge. If I think in English, what will happen to me? Will I become another person?

It. The flame of immobility. I can see it, it consumes me. The language-machine brings me closer and closer to formalizations of a purely mathematical order. I command the void to stand at attention. When I was a programmer, I found myself swept up in a vast, warm storm of concepts. I breathe through my nose, because of the cavity in my tooth, which is sensitive to air. I breathe through my mouth, because of my stuffed-up nose. I don't breathe at all but walk very quickly, holding my breath, fists clenched in the pockets of my buckskin jacket, lips pinched about an imaginary cigarette, the habit of an ex-smoker. Pressed against the palm of my hand is the butt of my revolver. My heart pounding, I enter the bank. Then I turn and abruptly leave, making a mental note of the three steps from the door to the sidewalk, and circle the building. A fire escape in the back climbs the red brick wall like a number of superimposed Z's.

Back at the hotel, I play with the automatic. My throat is raw. I have a sudden thirst for beer. I toy with the thought of summoning a call girl: high vinyl boots, short skirt. I gaze at the veins in my hand: intricate trails of blood. In vain, I attempt to give myself up to the workings of chance, I cannot find the rhythm that will allow me to live each moment for itself, I'm always a little behind everyone else. What I want more than anything is to return to a state of original purity, as will exist after the extinction of the last coal on the last funeral pyre.

How am I to rid myself of this most recent obsession? If I'm caught, it will mean how many years in prison? My God, I'm losing control of myself! I've brought so much pressure to bear on my existence, in an attempt to alter its course, that I've actually become delirious.

I get up and look around for the time, then remember there is no clock in this room. I dress: jeans, black turtleneck, sandals. I hang my jacket over my arm, in such a way as to allow me easy access to the pocket that holds the revolver. I step through the open glass doors leading onto the balcony. In the garden, the fringes of a parasol flutter in the wind. Standing before the glass, I hide the lower half of my face beneath the rolled neck of my shirt, making sure I can turn my head in all directions without revealing my identity. The sweat is streaming down my body. Once again, I study the map of the neighborhood. It won't be any easier this time than on the two previous occasions: the closed door, the armed guard. A delivery boy from the corner grocer emerges from the neighbor's house, counting his change, and straddles his bicycle. Yesterday, I sold my camera to pay for a meal in a restaurant.

An F-18 fighter plane, probably from an air force base down the coast, passes overhead, trailing a mountain of thunder in its wake. On Sunset Boulevard, a prostitute bites into a hot dog, gobs of yellow mustard trickling between her firm, heavy breasts, their contours clearly delineated by her tight-fitting bikini top.

The dancelike movements of the gulls demonstrate the existence of a third dimension than remains forever inaccessible. Everything will be taken from me. The wind rattles the yellowed fronds of the palm trees.

***

Gone? My homeland? Never. Not unless I cut off my tongue. The chrome on the cars glitters in the LA sunlight. I've had enough of this. I want to see the snow again, to trudge through the slush. All this cold chaff, this inescapable cup of anguish. I shall go back to processing data at the Centre, I shall swallow my daily dose of video, I shall turn myself over to the ADN and its circumstantial discourse.

No, I have no choice but to go on. I switch on my portable multiband receiver, giving me instantaneous access to all the police channels in the city. Voices reach my ears, interspersed with bursts of static. The phrases follow one another erratically, punctuated with numbers. I have managed in the past to decipher such enigmatic reports. There is no code that cannot be cracked by a conscientious programmer. Accuracy is attained through the use of the right reading grid. Before making my move, I shall wait until the patrolmen are called out of the neighborhood to deal with another holdup.

"A name to be verified. . . responding to a 2-43, perhaps a 10-21 . . . there's no need to be arrogant… do you have a car in the vicinity of Wilshire Boulevard?...208, I'm on my way...0-79, Santa Monica Boulevard, car out of gas in the service lane. . .10-14, stabbing victim on Sunset…I'll be right there, I'm in the vicinity of Hollywood Drive...yes, I can see you behind me."

Seated on my balcony, I watch a woman in hair curlers enter the bank on the corner of the street. The smoke from a distant blast furnace climbs into the molten silver sky. On the sidewalk, a little boy plays baseball with an imaginary ball, striking the air repeatedly with his bat, then repeating the gesture in slow motion, like a television replay. Though the sky is overcast, the light striking the fronts of the houses is intense, lending the bricks a sensual, almost carnal, hue. In the fish market, a clerk severs the head and the tail of a trout with two swift, precise blows of his knife, then wipes his bloody hands on his apron.

The blasting of car horns, the odors of frying food, the shadows of clouds passing over a newsstand creating the illusion that the stand itself is moving: each impression takes me by surprise, its strangeness, its wildness, its...

"Central to all cars. Two armed suspects have just fled northward on route 295."

I race down the stairway and across the street. The first drops of rain strike my face. Sirens wail in the distance. I take a firm grip on the gun, turn my collar up to my eyes and push open the big glass doors.

Everyone freezes at the sight of me, knowing what the slightest movement might mean. When I've emptied all the tills, I turn back to the door. A guard stands with his arms at his sides, gazing at the floor. He had me at his mercy during the entire holdup. I didn't even know he was there. At any moment, he could have pulled his gun and shot me in the back.

I run toward the alley, glancing over my shoulder to be sure I'm not being followed, then make my way to the rear door of the hotel. Fortunately, I don't encounter anyone while climbing the stairs. As I slide the bolt in my door, I glance at my watch: scarcely two minutes have passed. I close the balcony window to shut out the ringing of the alarm. I stretch out on the couch and light the cigar I promised myself if I pulled the job off successfully. I'll count the money later. I feel numb. Nowhere to go but here. Nothing here but now. Nothing now but here. And here is truly here. Like an aquatic plant in an agreeably tepid pool, I try to recall the faces of the people in the bank. But their features are blurred, as if I'd passed them on the run. On the receiver, I hear the announcement of yet another holdup, the robber fled in an unknown direction. The trash collectors are making their habitual racket in the street, emptying trash cans into the hungry maw of the truck, its belly rumbling contentedly with each gulp.

***

All existence is empty. There is neither illusion nor the cessation of illusion. I allow the joy of success to permeate me. In a toilet at the airport, before boarding the plane for LA, I tore up all my ID cards: a cloud of white confetti carried away by the swirling water. Since then, I have ceased to be, like a dream banished forever by a cup of strong coffee and the morning newspaper.

I sink the syringe into the filter tip of a cigarette. Then, taking a minute quantity of heroin, I inject it with a quick, deft movement just below the right bicep. Then I pull gently on the pump. I know that I have aimed accurately when I watch the blood mount and mingle with the water. I press on the piston. The knots in my muscles loosen. A surge of sweet, singing energy transforms my body into a strange, new object, relieved for the moment of all responsibility. Death is only an idea, which renders possible all other ideas. I stop analyzing myself. I belong totally, irrevocably, to myself. My pupils dilate. Now, I can shut myself off from the others, perceive them as objects. I laugh. The drug has caused my voice to descend an octave. I think of Carly, and desire for her climbs between my thighs. I'm still waiting for her call. I must find her again, must speak to her with word-cords that will restrain, link, embrace.

There seems no further possibility of rational thought: an image moving like a mirror down a highway. But I have not applied any silvering to the back of my conscious mind, for I do not wish to see reflected there the gloomy succession of wasted days.

The rattling of the palms in the wind outside my window sends shivers up my spine. A pedestrian hastens through the rain, illuminated for a moment in a set of headlights that cause his shadow to lengthen, then shorten. The clouds bang in a thick, solid mass over the city, a leaden lid beneath which distances are compressed. Leaning on the windowsill and breathing on the glass, I draw suns in the steam, the bundles of bills piled in my lap as light as a purring kitten.

SMOG

A strike! I smile, turning to the girls in the next lane, my thumb raised in a sign of victory. Someone makes an erratic throw: there is the crash of a ball dropping into the gutter. With three gins in my gut, what do I care if I don't know where I'm going? In the end, I won't budge an inch, either literally or figuratively. This thought calms me.

"Did you throw that ball, miss?"

When I reach the point of no longer giving a damn, my apathy often produces miracles. I take her by the waist and escort her out to the parking lot. Seated with her in the back seat of my Chevrolet, I suddenly break into tears, just like an imbecile. She gazes at me incredulously, apparently under the impression that I planned to engage in a different sort of release, but, good girl, she consoles me, caressing the head that rests on her breast.

"Excuse me, but I had a teacher once who said you should cry at least once a day. If not, the tear ducts will become blocked and you'll end up with a terrible headache."

She shakes her head in bewilderment. Suddenly her two companions appear, calling her name. I ask her to stay. She says: another time. So destiny will head me elsewhere in this city of LA.

I decide to stop at a club. The drum ceases abruptly. Standing in the center of the stage, the naked dancer raises her arms in the air, teeth bared, eyes half-closed, in a simulation of passion. My brain must be playing tricks on me. No one could possibly have pronounced my name. No one but... No, it's just another illusion. I set my glass down and gaze at the walls, which stretch away in every direction.

The principal artifice of the detective consists in imitating the actions of his prey, in becoming for a time his reflection, his echo, in infiltrating his company so slowly and so subtly that the victim pays him no more heed than he does his own shadow. I decide to drive at random for a while, in the hope of ridding myself of a possible pursuer.

A sign posted by a left-wing group states: Make The Rich Pay.

The gardeners of Beverly Hills cut the grass on the steep lawns with mowers attached to long cables. Holes in the asphalt are surrounded by yellow trestles with black diagonal lines, bearing the caution: No Parking. I pass a family of campers returning to town, a canoe on the roof of the car. A couple flees the burst of machine-gun fire from a pneumatic hammer. A man who resembles a Spanish count with a gray goatee, but who is in fact a street sweeper, pushes a crushed Coke can and an empty cigarette pack down the street. Before a bed of flowers, bright candies on a paper velvet lawn, stands the statue of a peasant with a book in his hand. A sign in the window of a furniture store proclaims: The Time Of Certain Values Has Arrived.

A child stands peeing on a Rolls-Royce. Clouds of dust from an excavation site rise about the wheels of passing buses, their windows looking like big sad eyes. A woman in a blue suit emerges blithely from a funeral parlor with tinted gray windows. A passer-by is almost knocked off his feet; he steps deftly aside, like a toreador evading a charging bull. The trees are green cotton-candy on twisted poles. I ate too fast: there is a big lump in the pit of my stomach. The windshield wipers slap to and fro, saying: no, no, no. The patter of the rain on the roof of the car sounds like chicken frying in a pan. A man stands motionless at the entrance to an underground garage, like a figure painted on the concrete wall; perhaps he will dissolve in the downpour. The tightness of throat, the micro-deception, before each red light. An old man with a beard leans over a washing machine in a Laundromat, counting his change. Two squirrels cross Doheny Street on the run, paying no heed to the corpse of their little brother on the pavement. A cat follows them, its body pressed tightly to the ground. In Long Island Port, little sailboats move up on a departing Soviet steamer. A Chinese woman in oilskins clasps an Iron Man lunchbox to her chest. Viewed from this angle, the spires of Holy Sacrament Church look like diabolical horns.

From having repeatedly traced the same route, I recognize certain faces. Telling myself that no one would have the courage to follow me like this for two whole hours, I enter Forest Lawn Cemetery and stop near the big mausoleum containing the remains of W. C. Fields, Jean Harlow and Clark Gable. The closed curtains of an open-air theater contain two large religious murals, one depicting the Crucifixion, the other, the Resurrection, both the work of Jan Styka. A family of Mexicans emerges from a chapel, where they have just witnessed a marriage ceremony. I advance among the tombs, hoping to escape any indiscreet gaze, and stop before the stone that bears the inscription I am seeking: MARC FRECHETTE, 1947-1975. The modesty of the monument, the absence of flowers, the presence of weeds, all testify to the fact that no one has visited the site for a long while. With the knife I brought for this purpose, I remove a small rectangle of grass and dig into the earth with my bare hands. In the niche thus formed, I place the $18,900, tightly sealed in cellophane. Then I carefully replace the earth and the turf, smooth the grass with my hand and step back to check the effect: nothing to betray my work. I wipe my fingers on my handkerchief, silently asking Marc Frechette to keep watch over the money I'm lending him interest-free. As for Kelp, by this time tomorrow he should have the money order for $4000 I put in the mail for him a short while ago.

***

Today, I called my wife. The moment she heard my voice, she began to shout. Her words buzzed in my head like a swarm of angry bees, their very contact causing me pain. They swept out of the receiver and traveled throughout my body, along the nerves, through the vital organs, biting, stinging, subjecting me to the various stages of her emotional appeal. I kept telling myself that they were just sounds, that they couldn't hurt me, that

I no longer understood the language she was speaking, but they struck a nerve deep in my quivering flesh, causing it to turn in on itself in a desperate attempt to flee the horror of existence, incapable of escaping those phrases that resounded in my ear like explosions. I placed my head in my hands, my legs drawn up to my chest. Finally, I succeeded in shutting off her noisy tirade. But then I was struck with the fear of dying. And my panic lent me the strength to end the call, without another word. It was several minutes before I regained consciousness of my surroundings.

***

I press my hands tightly to my abdomen. Standing on the carpet, rocking to and fro, brow furrowed, eyes closed, I try to observe my pain calmly and objectively, telling myself that it will pass. But it's getting worse. My breathing accelerates, and suddenly I find myself gasping. I moan beneath the shock of the attack. In vain do I tell myself: it's nothing, just a moment of fleeing anguish, it doesn't really hurt. In this way have I repeatedly denied the reality of my feelings, attributing them to something as simple as indigestion. I can see now that there has never been a moment in my life when I wasn't in pain. I yell with rage at my apparent inability to put an end to my existence, furious with the others for what they have inflicted upon me. Plunged into the cold, dark wilderness of non-love, I hammer the floor with such violence that, when I rise to my feet, I observe that my knuckles are bleeding.

I remain absolutely still, trying to summon the strength to face the imminent night. For it cannot be escaped, unless I manage to transform myself into a god with a stone mask. Like water, my eyes repeatedly assume the form of whatever receives them. I let myself go, right to the tips of my trembling lips, where death slumbers. I shall talk and talk until the words follow clearly upon one another, no longer resisting the world but superimposing themselves upon it. Despite their countless interpretations, they all have the familiar color of my voice.

I recall my daughter's braids: two little antennas rising on either side of her head, bent toward the TV set to pick up its mysterious electronic waves, while outside the snow swirls about the houses. Another time: she and her brother, dressed alike in white sweaters with red stripes, velvet shorts and canvas booties, are standing beside the car in the driveway, hugging each other. I've just mowed the lawn: the aroma of cut grass mingles in my nostrils with the smell of my cigarette. My shadow lies over the asphalt.

And yet again: my son is standing with a plastic airplane clutched between his legs, its propeller driven by an elastic band. In his wagon, which is attached by a long cord to his tricycle, lies a hammer. He's wearing a cap bearing the insignia of a famous baseball team. His sister is eating popcorn. It is a lovely day. At the bottom of the nearby ravine flows a torrent of water. In the aviary of the zoo, a bald eagle gazes calmly at us.

I make good my escape, moving flush with the ground, between the legs of the ants. The spray of the ocean waves is iridescent in the sunlight. The forest of sequoia trees is crisscrossed with narrow trails, faint scrawls on a green mat.

Where is Carly hiding? It is as if I were packed in ice. I feel nothing, from head to toe. I have attained the state of absolute zero. What must I do to regain the use of my senses? Total refrigeration of the universe. I want all the suns of California to assemble themselves about me. I must abandon all hope, for I am about to force my way back into the womb. Deep in my own thoughts, I have discovered the presence of the perennial enemy: the father.

Perhaps I should slip quietly back? I no longer can

see anything in my head. The sounds coalesce, acquire texture, color, and become paintings: a total synthesis that permits my sentiments mount in resounding echoes to my brain. I remember now: she was dancing in the middle of the trail. What am I going to do with my thing-a-ma-jig? I'm approaching the end, what more can I say? I can't think and think at the same time. I don't love her. I don't love anyone. No one loves me. A good beginning for a suicide note, the authenticity of which could be verified from the frequent recurrence of the word *love*.

I know that I am capable of even greater suffering, that there is no limit to what a human being can endure. Pushing my cowboy hat to the back of my head, I shift my gaze slightly, my brows knitted above the fixed, expressionless, green eyes, my shoulders partially concealing the hill behind me on which giant letters spell out: H-O-L-L-Y-W-O-O-D. I pass my fingers slowly over the three-day stubble on my face. There is no reason to go on suffering like this. I could at least put an end to the cacophonic flock of sensations and sentiments that has appeared out of nowhere to assault me, assuming identifiable forms, producing articulated sounds, flying about madly for a few moments in the night before disappearing again.

An invisible line bisects LA into two identical halves, both possessing the same habitations and the same pedestrians simultaneously turning the same street corners. But I notice that the people in one half don't speak quite the same words as their counterparts in the other half. Language constitutes the only point of reference in this stereoscopic city. So I must choose between the two statements I utter at any given moment.

I swing my arms forcefully to and fro, blow like a furnace, burst into laughter, puff out my chest, accelerate the circulation of my blood, mimic my own voice. And the words flow from my mouth: *eins, zwei, drei*. The volume grows and grows deep in my throat. Lock the door. The police may attempt to break into the room like I-don't-know-what into my consciousness.

The city is blanketed in smog. Clusters of terrestrial stars on the black asphalt: little tentacular puddles that will evaporate in the sun. The moon is shining in the hung-over dawn. The three TV sets in a store window show a shot of an altar-piece. The end of the world is unfolding through a very prosperous death agony. Time is speeded up, the seconds rain all about me. Only an extreme concentration allows me to move through this constantly changing landscape, with no clear points of departure or arrival.

Change of speed. The victory of solipsism manifests itself in millions of particles that assume the form of my mother, microscopic doll guarding beneath her scintillating cloak the highly divisible members of the species.

Now, I'm walking down a shady lane lined with high trees. Flowers are spots of bright light on clipped lawns. I enter the apartment. Carly is wearing a large sombrero she bought in the Mexican quarter. She leads me to the bed. Her singing voice lulls me to sleep. When I'm completely relaxed, I find myself willing her to squeeze the trigger upon which my index finger is posed. But you won't dare, my angel, you're going to leave me to face that final explosion alone.

***

On the black ceiling of her room, she has pasted stars of fluorescent cardboard to form the signs of the zodiac. When she wants to escape from herself, all she has to do is focus her attention on the designs above her head. Does she find my unhappiness an irresistible attraction, like a zone of shadow she would like to illuminate? We are so completely different. I couldn't care less about the others. All I want to do, in the light of my returning consciousness, is to think of her. For her, the world is governed by sentiments, which lend it relief and perspective. She cries in movies, while reading poetry, while listening to me. . . or the hockey player. . . or the waitress at Mister Donut. And her sadness at such moments is not something she tries to escape. The only thing she fears is the possibility one day of feeling nothing at all. There is nothing of the pious saint about her: she makes love voraciously, her legs clasping my flanks, her blue eyes rolling back in her head, like an epileptic. And she sometimes has rages that alarm me, shrieking like a wild cat, as she did the time she found the syringe I use to shoot up with and smashed it to pieces. But, at her contact, I sometimes feel that it might be possible for me to love all things, not at some distant time and place, the culmination of some long-awaited discovery, but here and now. At such moments, I'm like a man struggling to hold onto a dream, his head stuffed beneath the pillow, his hand groping for the alarm clock to silence its incessant ringing. Sitting cross-legged before the fireplace, she smears her face with soot, then, picking up her guitar, says in the drawling accents of a black woman: "With yo' permission, sir, I'll sing the blues."

One evening, as we emerge from the Chinese Theater, I ask Carly if she'd like to live in the desert.

"Why?"

I explain to her that I must drop out of sight for a while. Otherwise, I'll never succeed in shaking off my past. My former employers think I absconded with some secret documents. It's only a matter of time before they come in search of me.

"You're going to run away again?"

"Not so far this time. I want to buy a piece of land in the Mojave Desert, a hundred acres or so."

"And what about my work? I'd be bored to death."

"We'd have TV."

Carly's laughter prompts a gardener watering tulips in front of a colonial-style mansion to glance our way. I feel a little foolish, but though the irony of my suggestion clearly did not escape her, I sense that she is not entirely displeased by the proposal.

''I'd have to give up my dreams of becoming an actress, at least for a while," she says, and adds that she'll think about it.

That's all I ask. Meanwhile, I tell her, I want her to return to Santa Monica. I'll call her the moment everything is settled. Then we'll organize her disappearance.

"Will I have to change my name?"

I nod. I'll find her a new identity in the computer.

"And will you be happy out there among the cactus?"

"Why not? I like silence."

We pass by a tennis court, where two women are playing and cursing each missed shot, their mouths full of chewing gum. We enter a restaurant, where a waitress informs me that the ice cream is sold at the next counter, she handles only hot food. I place the order and am given a number, which will be called over a microphone when it is ready.

We eat outside, seated on a sand pile in a vacant lot. Cawing crows dive among the spruces. I spy a dead cat in the middle of the road: it looks as if it had exploded.

"I can't go to Santa Monica," says Carly, avoiding my gaze. "I'm leaving for Finland tomorrow with the goaltender. He's playing the role of a soldier on skates in a movie set on a frozen planet. It seems they believe in other galaxies over there. He persuaded them to let me go along. He's going to introduce me to the crew."

With a dead branch, I scrawl the name Marc Frechette in the sand, then erase it with my shoe, then begin all over again.

"I can't refuse. There's even a chance I may be taken

on as an extra. Besides, I think he suspects I'm seeing someone behind his back. This is the first time he's offered to take me along with him. The neighbors must have seen you at his place and told him. We'll discuss your project when I return. If you're still around, that is. You're a difficult man to love, you know. And there's such an emptiness in you the moment you stop talking, I'm afraid of you at such moments."

I pile stones over my feet: little, big, white, pink, yellow, spotted, marbled, veined, polished, rough, angular, round, pointed....I recall a stone I saw in a Vermont museum, on which the scene of a shipwreck had been etched, not by human hands but by nature itself. Bidding Carly farewell, I wonder how many billions of years of abrasion and erosion and corrosion it would take to reproduce that lovely face, which I shall not see again for three long weeks.

Radio-Void

To be completely aware of LA would require a mathematical recklessness that I am incapable of exercising at the moment. I have moved into a tiny apartment at the top of a thirty-story building, the single window of which looks out on the Pacific. Arriving in a straight line from Japan, the wind whistles between the parallel steel bars of the balcony railing, playing a sad concerto. In this setting of concrete and steel, so cold that it sets my teeth to aching, among these sticks of rented furniture, I continue to pry beneath my eyelids, to excavate the tunnel of the great evasion all the way to my larynx, which keeps time at the moment to the tapping of my fingers. But the world imposes itself upon me too violently and too rapidly to allow me any such freedom. The cord of the ventilator rattles against the metal slats, sending shivers up my spine.

I observe those who converse in my head. A thousand different voices, chanting to the accompaniment of multiple searing beams of light. What I say is never in keeping with what can be said. The beauty of jet planes darting through the evening sky fast enough to escape the night. Symptom of hara-kiri: painful median line. It blows on the heights of my incurable head. Will the letters eventually get the better of my thought?

A world from which the word would be absent, that could be grasped in its entirety, without shadings or nuances, its contours clean and sharp, as if cut with the fin of a shark. The contradictions, the contractions, the itchings, the spasms, all these provoke the resurgence of reality, which a simple yawn will propel back into the void. The skater suddenly finding himself in a puddle of water. Fancy figures, skate figures.

My mental circuits gasp for breath, like exhausted steeds that have climbed countless hills to bring news of the hero's exploits. The latter has had himself committed to prison, following an inquiry into his failure to obey some obscure algebraic law. Every evening, following recreation, the prisoner-guard with the enormous mustache paces to and fro in the courtyard, dragging his saber in the dust.

Things disintegrate in the light. To understand is to annihilate the primeval night. I walk along multiple routes, which constantly change altitude without advancing or retreating: space is a held breath. The sun, precious angel, induces a certain monotony. All I have to do is remain here in my room till midnight to become transparent. The crisis preceding the world. That epileptic seizure teaches me more than all the known formulas.

Perhaps, as a result of augmenting my ignorance, I shall end up learning something. The sky slides down my esophagus. Body to body with the delirious speed of the Saint, the accursed goddess of my pale nights. Carly, I hate you. I press my feet firmly to the floor. Up through the crepe soles of my shoes, up through the numerous floors of the building, I feel the matricidal earth. It commands me to undress, to rub my forehead in the dust. The Centre would like me to become a corpse manipulated by spider threads, in the void of this city.

The ninny in the next room tapped me on the wrist this morning, a gesture for which I fervently pray he may impale himself on a 7-Up bottle. I try to follow my breathing, which beats to the cosmic measure of my flight into the microscopic distances. The floor is a plain, a plaint. The shred of wool I swallow leaves an impression of infinite softness against my palate. The taste of bread I know. But what of the taste of air, trees, asphalt? What of the taste of the void?

LA wants to swallow me up, but I still have the fury to resist it. Nothing can surprise me anymore. I already know the shape of all the experiences that await me. The tribunal had better not beat about the bush when dealing with the likes of me. I have deserved the pox and the stocks a hundred times over. Lead me to the gallows without further delay.

Outside, the smog has sullied the sky. I go down to the restaurant, gasping for breath, thinking of those poor blacks who committed suicide on American slave ships by swallowing their tongues.

I slavishly lap up my soup, my elbows cramped by my two companions. I sense directly the violence exercised by my conscience upon my undifferentiated erotic ardor. I have an inkling of the extreme happiness that would be mine if I ceased being a moral creature. The reduction that precedes the appearance in the mirror, which precedes the expansion, has already begun. Soon my body will slip into the clarity of total illusion, and will remain fixed there till the end of the seven mandatory years of woe.

***

I drive through LA, a city engulfed in the cold flames of countless TV sets, listening to Radio-Void and its automatic distribution of inconsequential messages. In Kansas, birds that swallowed an industrial poison are laying rotten eggs on the hats of scarecrows. Prices have gone up, but you can still buy a pound of salmon for $9.99; as for oysters, it's best to wait. Intermittent sunshine and heavy smog are forecast for Tuesday and Wednesday. The Pasadena Expressway has been cleared, but Interstate 95 is still blocked. The house descends toward me as I approach the summit of the hill. I struggle against drowsiness, against the hypnotic trance of stippled tapes. In the distance, clouds rise from the fiery cauldron of the mountains.

The movement doesn't stop when I reach my room. Might as well make use of it, let myself be carried by the current. Carly has assumed the form of some indeterminate object that I am obliged to identify. If I make a mistake, I will be punished by being obliged to place my penis in the demon's miniature guillotine. The blade falls but nothing happens. It didn't work. *What is this, then?* asks the executioner, placing a sausage-like object in the palm of my hand. On the CBS network, I observe a cybernetic monster of black plastic with a raspy voice: the inauguration of this planetary base marks an important stage in the growth of our galactic empire.

Carly should be back by now. I call her at the stadium, to avoid having to speak to the goaltender. Unable to conceal her excitement, she arranges to meet me tomorrow morning at Universal Studios: the lobby of Building H-2. She has great news for me! I decide to pass the evening at the gym, lifting weights. At one point, I manage a clean-and-jerk of 225 pounds. Nothing calms me more than this struggle against gravity. When you see things in terms of their weight, your thoughts weigh less heavily on you, almost everything proves to be immutable.

The earth always ends up reclaiming what I take from it, whether an iron weight or my own body. Wiping myself down, I discover that someone has stolen the wedding ring I placed on the bench so it wouldn't cut into my finger. Joelle bought that ring for me in Rhodes; she had my name engraved inside the band. When we emerged from the jeweler's shop, we were confronted by a young hippie who had eluded the municipal by-law against begging by hanging a cup around the neck of his dog with a sign that read: Do You Have Some Spare Change I Can Lend My Master? I threw a few drachmas into the metal container.

"It'll bring you luck," said the young American, winking.

"That's right," said Joelle with a laugh. "You'll never lose this ring."

And now an absurd sadness takes hold of me, like the time my father broke my kite over his knee:

"This is one missile that won't get tangled up in my TV antenna again!"

My real name is recorded nowhere. I wonder how much longer I will remember the one who used to say *I* in another language. I-vampire, I-martyr, I-phantom, I-word, I-silence. I which has become he: Marc Frechette.

***

The talk goes on and on, day and night. All I have to do is turn the dial and the LA choir reaches my ears, interspersed with bursts of spitting and crackling:

"206 to LA...Metro... Go ahead... Call San Diego for further instructions...We have no description of the two men.

"Do you think they escaped?...We find him customers,

he pays us...10-4, he'll probably return to the bar, join us there.

"I'm on my way...1070 Wilshire, reports of a sick customer. Go to 1258 Hollywood, ask for John Capinostro, date of birth: 7-10-79; warrant number: 42-32.80... She was reported missing 29 November, wearing slacks, dark sweater, black hair... Another one? Aren't you ashamed?...I'm not here long on the weekends, so I have to work fast...Striana Street? No, it doesn't exist...What about your friend, Mike?

"He's still alive...Was the vehicle heading north or south?

"West, it proceeded from Cherry to Bellflower... I didn't see it pass, it must have gone down Lakeshore the wrong way."

NOSFERATU

The profusion of prison-like towers that stand in tight granite ranks in the city's core. The straight line of history leads infallibly to LA, cast from the same mould that all the world's cities strive to emulate, cancerous growths of concrete, asphalt and steel dotting the earth's surface. I should like to ride horseback down the streets of this *fin-de-siècle* setting, a simple cowboy in search of his origins. With my syringe, I tat a daring lacework of snow and frost on my arm. My breathing accelerates and a drop of sperm strikes the red tiles of the balcony, thirty stories above the head of the prostitute I have been observing through the binoculars. To say nothing, not now, not ever. The silence of the old immigrant who cannot find his way back home. More and more alone and lost in the world.

To discover that which is not self-evident. That which blocks, chafes, crushes. To dismantle one's own imposture, step by step. And if there are nothing but appearances, if there are no depths, if I exist only in movement? Things toss, turn, dissolve, will not remain still. There are no final explanations, neither in this world nor in the next. No shadows. Nothing but light. I am wasting away, like a computer being consumed by an electronic tapeworm. The end of my story is fast approaching. I can no longer make any distinctions, the people about me live in a state approaching absolute zero. I must at least learn to love them a little, to lend them a little life. If not, the game is up. I shall be able to evaluate myself only in regard to my combustibility on the day of the thousand suns. Six times this year, deep in the Cheyenne Mountains, the computers of the air force station have issued false alarms. I must locate the roofs of the missile launching sites. Then, ensuring that the attack-codes correspond to the combinations of the safes and making a supreme effort not to think, I shall pull the switch. Right to the end, the radio will continue to play rock music.

LA hardly changes in appearance from season to season, from street to street, from day to night. Time has stopped here, like a video playing endlessly on a screen of dreams erected on the Pacific shore. Whether one is in California or Montreal, LA is a nodal point that reflects all history. The boulevards go nowhere: I am stupefied by the monotonous repetition of McDonald restaurants, KFC outlets, motels, gas stations, the reduction to clouds of carbon monoxide and speed of sources of energy that took thousands of years to come into being.

***

The doors of the elevator open. Carly steps out and embraces me.

"I've got great news! I have an audition in three days!"

I hand her a notebook and ask for her autograph. Laughing, she searches in her purse for a pen. Finding none, she borrows one from the receptionist, who tells her to keep it as a good luck charm. She writes: To my sweet Québécois.

We stroll through the largest image-factory in the world. From one set to the next, the places and periods follow each other in a disorderly fashion. Carly tells me that she was taken on as an extra, just as the goaltender had promised. She skated on a frozen lake in Finland, wearing the improbable outfit of an astronaut. The action took place on a planet entirely covered with snow, where the temperature was gradually cooling, killing off the last of the inhabitants, who waited in vain for a spaceship from Earth.

"It must be a little like your country," she says.

I ask her what role she's auditioning for.

"Nina, in a remake of *Nosferatu*. And I'd be very grateful if you'd help me rehearse my lines."

While she gives me details of her trip, I lead her down several short deserted streets to be sure we're not being followed. A sign in front of a motel on Sunset Boulevard says: No Fins In Our Pool.

A young black man passes by on a bicycle, the front wheel raised high in the air, the handlebars wrapped in tiger skin. A taxi driver blasts his horn and beckons to a friend waiting for the bus. I wonder about the purpose of the huge cast-iron pipes attached to the front wall of a fire station: are they to bring water gushing into the emergency reservoirs of the fire engines? A brawny fireman twists a nut onto the enormous bolt of a hydrant. I park near the tower in which I live. Carly points to a mannequin in a store window: the woman is wearing a pencil skirt and a silk blouse and standing with her arms outstretched, as if appealing to an invisible audience.

"Whether they're real or plastic," says Carly, "the models are all the same."

I shake my head in disagreement. "I find your model

unique."

She says she's anxious to put my sincerity to the test. Without further delay. We take the elevator to the roof terrace. From here, we can see the myriad lights of the city reflected in pools and lakes and ocean; lights, disposed in parallel horizontal and vertical lines, twinkling across Hollywood, Beverly Hills, Westwood, Pasadena, Southeast and Southwest LA; individual lights and clusters of lights; sinuous and straight streams of light, all descending silently to the invisible beaches and the sea.

Stretching out on a lawn chair, Carly says to me:

"Nina has decided to risk her life to save her fiancé, Jonathan, and the city of Brême, which is being ravaged by the plague. She must keep Nosferatu at her side until dawn, when the first rays of the sun will destroy the vampire."

She asks me to stand behind the glass door at the top of the stairway. She lies back in the lawn chair, feigning sleep. Suddenly, she sits up, a look of horror on her face. I gaze silently at her. She places a hand on her left breast, then, throwing her head back, rises slowly from the chair. Her arms stretched before her like a sleepwalker, she approaches me and opens the door. Then she steps quickly to one side and retreats, her hands over her eyes, backing all the way to the railing. I remain impassively in the doorway. She gazes frantically about the city below her, looking in vain for help. I advance. Her eyes dilate in terror. Moving backwards, she strikes the lawn chair and lets herself drop into it. On her face, there is a mixture of horror and fascination, as my hand slowly climbs the length of her white dress and comes to rest over her heart. I close my fist. She flinches. My lips approach her throat, they nibble at it. At this moment, the first rays of dawn strike the glass façade of the skyscrapers, turning them a deep pink. I rise shakily to my full height, my left hand clutching my chest, desperate to flee the sun that is about to strike my face, hiding my head in the crook of my elbow. Very slowly, my image begins to dissolve. A thread of smoke rises from the terrace. Now, I am being gnawed by worms, reduced to a handful of dust. Farewell family, farewell parents, farewell friends, your hearts will grieve for me but I am rid of you at last. With death, everything comes to an end.

The next morning, we stroll between columns of royal palms, smiling and laughing. I hear the beating of wings about my head, in the light, fresh air which is permeated with the aroma of red and white camellias.

She agrees to call me in three days, the moment

the audition is over. Whatever the result, she'll tell the goaltender she's planning to leave him. Then we'll spend several days together on the piece of land I'm planning to buy in the desert.

The Interrogation

I saunter down the aisles of a department store. I probably wouldn't have noticed Kelp's mask-like face with its glassy eyes, if it weren't for the mirrors placed at various angles about the changing rooms, drawing space out toward a series of imaginary crossroads linking electric mixers and parasols, mechanical monkeys and lacy mannequins....I escape through a revolving door and try to lose my pursuer in the streets of LA. But it is not easy to shake someone off in these wide, geometrical avenues.

How on earth did he find me? He must have followed Carly to the studio where we'd arranged to meet. After all these weeks, I was hoping he might have abandoned the search. But I can see now that he'll never give up.

I spend a good half hour pushing my way through crowds, crossing intersections on red lights, entering the rear doors of movie houses, trying to alter my appearance by throwing off my jacket and pulling on a baseball cap, without knowing whether or not Kelp is still on my trail. Then I enter a bar. My nerves are shot and my stomach is in knots. I go directly to the washroom. Seated in a cubicle, my face beaded with sweat, I gaze at the floor, watching the tiles grow fuzzy. Through a crack in the door, I can see the urinals, little porcelain niches hardly big enough to conceal a man's penis. Some of them are blocked and emit foul odors, others run constantly and smell of disinfectant, like mysterious fountains exploding suddenly and enigmatically in powerful jets. Almost before I know what is happening, Kelp bursts through the door and strikes me on the head with the butt of his revolver. The effect is that of a frontal lobotomy performed without anesthesia.

***

The green eye is no longer a mysterious object. It's his watch, a lethal weapon, indestructible, irresistible: all but invisible. He is standing in the center of the room, as impassive as a figure in an engraving, his head rising stiffly out of the neck of his silk shirt. Somehow, he must have dragged me to his car without being noticed. Then, when he got me back here, he threw me on the bed and bound my wrists and ankles to the four posts. He approaches and leans over me, a bit of a smile on his face, a razor gripped in one hand. Very deftly, he reaches out and slices a strip of skin from my upper lip. Then he repeats the operation with the lower lip. The hot, acrid taste of blood fills my mouth, causing me to choke. I feel as if I'd pressed my lips to a flame. I try not to cry out, not to flinch, for I know that the slightest movement of my facial muscles will merely augment my pain. He disappears for a moment then returns with a pair of scissors. Placing my shrunken penis at the juncture of the two blades, he makes a slight incision on each side of the gland and says:

"Now, talk. Where's the money from the holdup?"

***

I know now what makes people kill: at such a moment, the death of another is the only way to put an end to one's suffering. I didn't know hatred could be so intense. In my case, it bears a closer resemblance to a raging toothache than to any other emotion. But I cannot cry out, I can't even weep, for I will only re-open my wounds.

***

I call Carly. There is no reply. I'll have to go to the stadium, to warn her of Kelp's threats. I profit from the darkness to pay a final visit to Marc Frechette's grave. As I expected, Kelp found the money, but he left my two grams of heroin wrapped in cellophane. I take a wreath from a nearby grave and lay it on Frechette's, in appreciation for his discreet, efficacious collaboration.

Back in my room, I chew up a couple of aspirins, while in the next apartment a woman yells: "And you have the nerve to come back and ask me for money, you useless fucker!"

I switch on my laptop and connect to the Centre. It's one AM in Montreal, the quietest moment of the day. I make contact almost at once. I compose the message. The reply appears on the screen: Your Code Please.

As a rule, I would respond by citing a number which, in keeping with a clearly established procedure, would allow me to obtain certain precise facts, though under no circumstances would I be given access to the ensemble of the semantic field, much less the ability to modify it. But because of my earlier interventions, all I have to do is write my name and I am granted not only immediate access to the memory bank but also the opportunity to add or subtract from the information stored in it. The computer can tell me almost anything, as long as I know how to phrase my request; otherwise, I will simply lose myself in the labyrinth of information, failing to distinguish between what is essential and what is not. And in the morning, with the arrival of the first personnel, my interventions will be detected at once. The authorities will have no choice but to suspend the operation of the computer, for I will exercise absolute control over all orders subsequently issued to it. They will have no choice but to scrap a machine that is worth millions of dollars.

My fingers fly over the keyboard, executing a melody of sense. Suddenly I am all-powerful, able to seize hold of things that are infinitely remote, to relocate myself anywhere in space and time. Somewhere between my neurons and all the computerized police files on the North American continent, a prodigiously rapid consciousness is born, probing the depths of its own entrails for information about a certain Kelp who works in the LA region, who measures about one meter-88cm and weighs about 90 kilos, and who is missing the index finger on his right hand.

A few moments pass, then a name and an address appear in luminous letters on the screen:

Henry Kelp, 245 Ocean Drive

Fortunately, Kelp left me my heroin. This will

allow me to remain impartial and lucid in the face of my suffering, which pervades me through and through, taking the form of toothaches, headaches, eye irritations, muscle spasms, sinus pains. I quickly inject myself with the contents of the syringe. But even before I withdraw the needle from the swollen vein in my arm, I realize that Kelp has replaced the drug with another mysterious white powder, whose effects I feel almost at once.

My conscious perceptions slow and come almost to a halt, I lose the thread of my thought, I can no longer get outside myself. Faced with a terrifying inquisitor, I dry up. I recall a cat we gassed in natural science class. Presuming it to be dead, the instructor removed the metal bell, prompting the animal to leap to the floor with a pitiful meow, leaving a small pile of excrement on the dissection table. Its heart pounding, its mouth flecked with foam, it collapsed beneath the blackboard. The thought crosses my mind that Kelp may have replaced the heroin with some deadly poison. Trembling, I tear open a carton of milk and gulp down its contents. But my mind continues to falter, my thoughts grow sluggish and disorganized. Whatever the drug is, it has channeled my powers of attention in unpredictable directions, as if it had discovered the password to my own inner programming. My breathing becomes irregular, spasmodic. I see a solid black mass in the back of my head, it's growing larger and larger, it's sucking me in, it's swallowing me up....I have lost all contact with myself....

PLAY-OFFS

The long blast of a car horn awakens me with a start. I'm seated at the wheel of my car, stopped at an intersection: the light is green. The driver behind me is impatient to proceed. My stomach is in knots and my head is spinning. I move ahead to let him pass, then pull over to the curb, adjacent to a park harshly lit by batteries of spotlights. A little league baseball game is in progress. My shoes are wet: I must have been walking through puddles or along the seashore. I remove one shoe and examine the sole: no trace of sand. My watch indicates 11:30 PM. So my blackout lasted nearly two hours. The knuckles of my right hand are scratched. I check my clothing: one shirt sleeve is torn. In one of my pants pockets, I find several hundred dollars cut into little pieces. My .45 is strapped to my hip. So, despite my somnambular state, I remembered to take everything Kelp might have laid his hands on during my absence. I drive at random through the streets, seeking out familiar landmarks. The neon sign over the front door of a bank says: Santa Monica.

So I'm not far from Bob's villa! Subconsciously, I must have wanted to go there, to warn Carly of the danger. I decide to follow through with this idea. I walk up to the front door of the house in which I spent two wonderful weeks and ring the bell.

"Come in, have a seat. What happened to your mouth? Someone hit you?"

I shrug. The goaltender gestures me to a seat in the living room. He has a black mustache and the fixed gaze of a cat. He tells me Carly is not home yet, we can wait for her together. She's working at the stadium tonight, so she shouldn't be late. She told him about me this afternoon.

"Of course, I knew she'd been entertaining a man here while I was away on the east coast. But I wanted her to bring the subject up herself. She couldn't go on shuttling between two lovers forever. Today, while we were preparing dinner, she told me everything. She said she's reached a decision."

"What decision?"

"I'd prefer she tell you that herself. Can I get you something to drink?"

I decline. I tell him I've followed all his hockey matches on TV. It's the best remedy for homesickness, a way of forgetting I'm in a foreign country.

"I like playing here," he replies. "It's quiet. When I played in Denver, we had to carry our own skates to and from the stadium. The owner had a trucking firm in Arizona. I drove a truck for him in the summertime, transporting dynamite. He used to give his players heart-shaped amphetamines."

I recall long evenings spent trying to decipher the enigmatic texts traced by skates, to unravel the mysterious significance of those flourishes and scrawls erased between each period by giant rotating brushes.

"Tomorrow, we're apt to be eliminated because the goaltender has had one drink too many," he says, draining his scotch in a gulp.

Scarcely audible cheeping sounds reach my ears from time to time.

"You hear that? Rats. The house is infested with them. I put poison out for them and now they're dying. But the little devils don't give up easily, spilling their guts and their blood all over the place. For some reason, the idea of being transformed into clean, dry, little mummies that won't pollute the atmosphere doesn't appeal to them."

Unable to conceal my uneasiness, I rise to leave.

"I think we should go and meet Carly at the stadium."

"Kelp threatened her again," he says with a smile. "The man is all bark and no bite."

I have no time to explain. I bid him farewell and leave. Ignoring red lights, I speed down the deserted streets of Santa Monica and onto the expressway that circles LA, moving in the direction of the Anaheim hills.

***

The stadium parking lot is empty, the big oval windows are dark. The game is over. At the entrance, a stout guard peers at me over his bifocals and tells me he didn't see Carly leave. He doesn't think she could still be in the building.

"What's that smell?" I ask him.

He sniffs and knits his brows. For a moment he stands there, perplexed, then whirls about and rushes toward a red metal door that leads to the wide corridor encircling the inner stadium. His big ring of keys rattling at his waist, he mutters:

"It's ammonia! The whole damn place could go up!"

I follow the old man down a spiral staircase leading to the machinery room. On a control board, two red lights are winking on and off in time to a ringing alarm.

Gasping for breath, the guard asks me to help him turn the crank to close the conduit leading from the main reservoir to the network of copper coils lying beneath the rink. My lungs are burning. A single spark, a minor short circuit, and this entire neo-classic structure will blow sky high, the Doric columns and plates of tinted glass and blocks of marble and ultramodern dressing rooms all rising into the sky, unfolding like the petals of a giant, poisonous flower beneath the smog-lid of LA, just like that villa at the end of *Zabriskie Point*, which the heroine imagines exploding with all its occupants inside.

Clutching his chest, the old man collapses against the wall. Barely able to speak, he points to a large roll of electric tape lying on a bench.

"Gotta stop up the pipe. . . up above. . .near the south net..."

Already, I'm running toward the spot he has indicated, checking with my thumb that the safety of my .45 is on.

And, everywhere, this pungent gaseous odor.

Emerging from the tunnel, I catch a glimpse in a plate glass partition of a man with -disheveled hair, green eyes and sun-darkened skin, wearing a navy blue suit and a red T-shirt. There is a dark stain in the crotch of his pants.

I push open the door in the boards and begin to run and slide toward the opposite end of the ice. Suddenly I perceive a yellow shape beneath the ice, at first vague and indistinct but growing larger and clearer as I approach it. My God... it's.... She's...lying there under the ice! She must have fallen, or she was pushed, and cracked her head on the copper pipe. Then the awful smell began to fill the building, as her blood made strange swirling designs in the slowly solidifying water.

I know now that I am going to kill Kelp.

This thought is engraved in my nerves, in my clenched fists, in the slits of my eyes that grow harder and harder.

Her mouth is open and there are lacerations all over her body. The knife pierced the throat between the sternum and the throat. Then he drew it out and plunged it into a less incongruous spot, the lower abdomen, just above the solar plexus, while she struggled in vain to wrench it loose, strange gurgling sounds escaping her lips. But it wasn't over yet. As the body continued to thrash about, the eyes silently pleading for mercy, he threw the knife aside and slowly strangled her, holding her head under the water.

She's still dressed in her usherette's uniform, with

its gold-fringed epaulets. Her right hand is protruding from the ice, and a light frost coats the delicate nails. Her wedding ring is missing: Kelp must have torn it off at the last moment, retrieving the final token of his disappointed love.

The eyes seized by the ice seem still to be gazing at the assassin bent over them. I kneel and try to kiss her on the lips. But I am left with the disturbing impression that I am embracing a mirror.

In the far corner of the rink, where gas is trickling out of the broken pipe, the water is bubbling and fizzing like soda pop. For a moment, I am tempted to abandon the guard to his fate and flee. But then I remove my shoes and socks and advance to the point where the water has not yet frozen.

He must have arranged to meet her here after the basketball game. Seated with her in the stands, he waited until all the employees had left, making one final attempt to persuade her to return with him, perhaps even showing her the money he's stolen from me. Then, when they were alone in the huge arena, inspired by the majestic setting, he led her out into the pool of water that was slowly filling the rink. She probably still didn't understand what he was up to. He may even have joked about it, saying with a laugh: "Come, let's go for a swim."

But when she gazed into his eyes, she must have

understood at last that she was going to play the long-awaited scene from *Nosferatu*, though without cameras or microphones or an admiring public this time. By now, it must have been a few minutes after midnight.

The pipe has given way at its weakest point, where it joins the main conduit. I mend it as best I can with the electric tape, obliged in the end to knot it. Gasping for breath, my head reeling, I lose my balance and for a moment have a vision of myself sinking into the bluish water, which is already beginning to congeal. But I reach out and steady myself against the boards.

I must get out into the open air.

***

My shoes have shrunk while drying, cramping my feet. The night is cool: I have to turn on the heater in my Chevrolet.

Judging by the darkened windows and the empty driveway, Kelp's house is deserted. I park several streets away and return on foot, forcing myself not to hurry. The waves breaking on the nearby beach sound like cars passing at regular intervals on the highway. A light fog envelops this section of Santa Monica. Moisture glistens on the dumbbells scattered about the enclosed outdoor gym, where each day the best body builders in California gather to flex their muscles for the benefit of incredulous onlookers. A sign in the darkened window of a restaurant advertises natural foods for the adepts of Muscle Beach. The sand crunches beneath my shoes as I make a tour of Kelp's bungalow, checking the windows for light.

It is here that Carly spent four years of her life, tending the rose bushes in front of the house, which are protected from the wind and rain by a low brick wall. Everything has become mechanical: my movements, the clouds rolling thick and dark beneath the moon, the palm trees lashed by the wind. All these things have lost their souls, just as I have lost Carly.

I feel so little that I actually find myself missing my suffering. I wrap my .45 in a handkerchief and smash the single pane of glass in the rear door. People rarely report suspicious sounds to the police. Even gunshots go unheeded, or are dismissed as the backfiring of automobiles. Most murderers remain at large, with the exception of those who confess through an excess of guilt. I am too familiar with the statistics to expect the law to avenge Carly's death.

On the table is a plate of pork chops, cooked but untouched, and a crushed beer can. Before leaving for the stadium, Kelp must have prepared a meal. He probably also took this opportunity to hide my money. Slowly and methodically, I search the kitchen, unconcerned about dirtying my hands and clothes, groping on my knees beneath the sink, opening containers, shaking out rags, tapping the walls and the floor. Then I move to the bedroom, where I tear open the mattress and pillows, look behind the paintings and examine the contents of the dressers, poking into the backs of drawers. In the living room, I run my hands over the two armchairs and the couch, then turn them on end, checking to see if the legs are hollow. Two hours later, I am back at the point of departure, empty handed. I'm shivering and my teeth are chattering: the effects of the massive dose of drugs absorbed earlier in the evening. And my throat is on fire. I raise the empty beer can over my head and shake it, hoping to catch a few drops. Nothing. And yet I sense that the container is not empty. I remove the top with a can opener. It is here, in this Schlitz can, that Kelp slid the bills, one by one, while his chops grew cold. I count them: only $300 missing. So I'll be able to buy my piece of land in Death Valley, after all.

Convinced that sooner or later Kelp will return home, I make myself as comfortable as possible in an armchair in the living-room. It's 3 AM. I feel drowsy.

The slamming of a car door awakens me with a start. It is daylight. I hear footsteps on the walk, then a key turning in the lock, and Kelp staggers into the room and collapses on the sofa, one leg hanging over the edge. He didn't see me. I wait for his breathing to grow steady, then approach him. He reeks of alcohol.

I switch on a lamp near his face. He merely groans, raising his right hand over his eyes to protect them from the overhead glare, revealing a wrist covered with deep scratches.

I know now that he killed Carly.

I remove the safety from my .45 and place the barrel close to his temple, disturbing a few of the bristling red hairs, raging at the knowledge that I am incapable of killing in cold blood.

Seizing his feet, I drag him from the couch to the floor. I kick him several times, surprised to discover that this man who spends several hours a day lifting weights is so soft and flabby. Several blows to the thighs prompt him eventually to open his glassy, bloodshot eyes, which look straight up into the barrel of the gun that gestures him to his feet.

He frowns. But realizing that he has no choice, he obeys, backing to the nearest wall and leaning against it for support. I avoid his gaze, afraid he may see in my eyes that it is I who am at his mercy.

"Empty your pockets!" I demand.

He throws to the floor a ring of keys, a wallet and a comb with several missing teeth, all of which I draw toward me with my foot and retrieve.

"Come," I say, indicating the door, "we're going to your office."

"Where's Carly? Isn't she back yet?"

Banishing the annihilating image that takes shape in my mind, I don't bother to reply. What he says is nothing, I tell myself. Just as he, too, will shortly be nothing.

I turn the knob and throw the door open, sending it slamming against the brick wall of the house. The violence of my gesture frightens Kelp, who backs quickly out the door. I hand him the keys, telling him to drive. I wait until he is behind the wheel before taking my place at his side.

On the expressway, the regular stream of commuters is flowing toward downtown LA.

A mile from the toll station where he works, I tell Kelp to park in the service lane. The roar of cars is deafening; the odor of carbon monoxide, stifling. I tell him to get out and continue on foot. Uneasy but glad to be rid of me, he opens the door a crack and slips to the front of the car. I wait till he has gone a few hundred feet down the highway before sliding behind the wheel. Each time a heavy vehicle passes, Kelp struggles to keep his balance, placing his weight on his right foot.

I think of the mathematical constant that determines the limits of certitude: my presence here and the hatred that inflates my heart, both of which have their source in a world of pure speculation, which is uncertain. I break into laughter at this thought, as I bear down on the accelerator.

Kelp hears me and whirls around. The Mustang is capable of attaining a speed of 60 mph in ten seconds flat. Anticipating that he will attempt to avoid me by leaping to the right, I turn slightly in his direction at the last moment. In the rearview mirror, I see him spin about, his arms raised in the form of a cross. Then a red pickup truck wings him, propelling him into the next lane, where another vehicle immediately strikes him and hurls him out into the center of the highway. He stands there for a moment, a strange, disjointed figure, a look of mute astonishment on his face. Then a sedan tears his arm off at the shoulder, causing the blood to gush from the socket like an exploding paint bomb. The battered body disintegrates, becomes the very antithesis of a solid, like helium liquefying in a laboratory. Kelp dissolves, disappears from the scene, the particles of his body transmitted suddenly and miraculously into a world of pure speed. Swiftly and methodically, the rush hour traffic eradicates all traces of his presence from the earth, though not a single driver perceives anything out of the ordinary.

DESERTION

We have placed Carly's ashes in a little box, with her name printed on the lid. The goaltender and I are in the garden, where several days ago she found a dead sparrow-hawk. We carry the little casket and the bird to a clearing carpeted with pine needles, some green, others already brown and dry, and dig a little hole, carrying out the wishes of the deceased. Carly wanted to be buried here, to be allowed to pass back into the earth and the roots of the trees, which will continue to stand here for many years yet, buffeted by sun and rain, snow and dew, moonlight and the scurrying feet of rodents.

The goaltender opens the box. The ashes are in a plastic bag secured by a yellow metal thread. Smiling, he pours them into the hole. A few are caught by the wind and blow away. A part of Carly hangs in the air before us. Then he tosses the sparrow-hawk on top of the ashes and adds a few dandelions. He marks the grave with a big stone.

So, a cycle is finished. Carly has left this world,

she no longer feels anything, she has "passed on." It is almost as if she had never existed, as if the very space she once occupied had vanished. In the little yard, each gust of wind tears a few more leaves from the ash tree. This morning, a neighbor has carried his concern for order to the point of knocking the last leaves from a shrub with his rake.

***

No psychology. I am a table, an old shoe, a giant ant eater. The tube holds me in its grip from morning till night. I forget why I ever came to this place. Despite the cramps and the emptiness, I know that I shall never leave. Though I don't cease moving, I remain at all times in the same spot.

A moment's hesitation and bzzz!, the fly has escaped. To catch it, one must act without thinking. I strike my hands together, as if I were cold and in danger of freezing to death. I cut each second up into thin slices. I don't dwell on anything. The motorcycle speeds along, without raising any dust; for the first time in months, it has rained in this part of the desert. There are patches of fog in the pass through the blue mountains. A bald eagle floats high over the giant *M* of a McDonald's sign, which stands on Plexiglas legs before the Santa Fe railway line. The ketchup has congealed in the bottom of the bottle.

Irritated, I pry it loose, then dilute it with a little water in my saucer, attempting to restore the coagulated sauce to its original consistency, unwilling to deprive myself of this indispensable ingredient to the perfect hamburger.

I turn the meat balls on the grill and open a can of beer. My feet resting on a pail, tipped back in my chair, I sing at the top of my lungs, certain that they will hear me all the way to Reno and Las Vegas.

I've bought myself a new cowboy hat, and with my three days' growth of beard and my Colt .45 semiautomatic slung on my hip, I must look like a real outlaw.